# FORCE
## OF THE
# DARK WOLF

**FORCE OF NATURE SERIES** BOOK 2

# KATHI S. BARTON

## Second Edition

This is a work of fiction. Names, characters, places, and incidents are products of the author's imagination or are used fictitiously and are not to be construed as real. Any resemblance to actual events, locations, organizations, or person, living or dead, is entirely coincidental.

# WCP
**World Castle Publishing**
Pensacola, Florida

Copyright © Kathi S. Barton 2012
ISBN: 9781938243899
First Edition World Castle Publishing July 15, 2012
Second Edition World Castle Publishing September 15, 2013
http://www.worldcastlepublishing.com

Cover: Karen Fuller
Photos: Shutterstock
Editor: Maxine Bringenberg

# CHAPTER 1

Gordon watched the women as they crossed the street. He'd been keeping an eye on Dark Treasures, the store they had been coming out of, for over a week now and was surprised at how much business the little shop seemed to do. When they disappeared into a car and drove off, he got out of his cruiser and walked over to the place.

He loved what the owner had done to the old building. The place had been an eye sore for several years...hell, probably as much as a decade. The new windows and the pretty flowers out front said, "welcome" in a way that his new sister-in-law CJ would say was good business sense. He just liked the way they smelled.

The window to the right as a person faced the building had a huge claw foot tub in it. The towels draped around it looked soft and fluffy...the white terry cloth looked like it was at least two inches thick. He smiled when he saw the array of rubber duckies all around the edge. The floor of the display was covered in baskets of soaps and bottles of what he thought might be bubble bath. His mom had some of the same things in the bathroom at the pack house. But what caught his eye were the bright gems hanging from

1

what seemed to be nothing, but was in fact fishing line. The glint of the gems sparkled in the afternoon light. The other window, the one to the left, was covered in brown paper and had the words "under construction" written in a bold hand.

The bell over the door announced his arrival into the establishment. "I'll be right out. Don't steal anything until I come out so I can at least take a good inventory of what you have."

Gordon looked toward the back where a curtain fluttered in the slight breeze. Someone, an older woman, spoke from the depths and he had to smile. He'd been under the impression that someone much younger ran the place.

"Hello. The cops, huh? Which one are you here for? I have four working today, but I'm betting it's the lot of them." She turned to look in the direction she'd come from as a ruckus came from the back. "Sounds like a herd of them, doesn't it?"

"Herd? No, I'm here to get something for my mother and my sisters. And to speak to the owner if that is possible. Would that be you?" She shook her head. "I'm Gordon Force by the way. And you would be...?"

"Oh, pardon me. I get so befuddled when I babysit for the kids. Some days it's like they suck me dry of energy, but I wouldn't have it any other way. Like just this morning, Sis wanted to know how to make a brew to get rid of the neighborhood boy. I told her that she'd have to ask her aunt. Besides, we aren't really witches as everyone says, just sell the stuff to make soaps and such. Her aunt is much better at that than me anyway. Then there was—"

"Aunt Glad." The softly spoken words had him turning toward the papered up display. "Why don't you just answer his questions and let him leave? We have to lock up soon and take the children home."

No one came out of the area and he looked back at who he assumed was Aunt Glad. She was smiling again. He wondered if she was always happy or if she was just trying to hide something. He started to ask her about what he'd really come for when the "herd" came through the curtained area.

The oldest—or he supposed he should say the tallest—was a pretty girl who looked like she had too much leg. Her golden hair hung down her chest in two fat braids that looked like she'd been through a briar patch and her hair had been pulled badly. He thought her to be a teenager or very close. The next two were boys of about eight and ten. He smiled at them as they tumbled into the room much like him and his twin did when they were in the mood for some fighting. The littlest, a girl of about five or six, came in behind the rest with her thumb in her mouth, and looked like she was mad, spitting mad. Gordon would bet his last dollar that she ruled the roost, and that she did so more like an adult than the child that she was.

"Aunt Glad, those two need to have a time out," the little girl said after popping the thumb out. "They knocked me over into the grass, and they both know how much I hate the grass."

"She was acting like a girl. She was stupid and when I told her, she threw a rock at me." The older of the two boys lifted his hair off his forehead and showed the aunt the golf ball-sized knot already there. "Then when it started to bleed she acted like it was the end of the world or something. Girls. Who the heck needs them?"

Gordon couldn't help it...he burst out laughing. He knew at that moment that they'd had no idea he was there until he did. Their eyes widened and the youngest was shoved behind the other girl while the boys took a stance in front of them. They were protecting each other. Gordon knew immediately that someone had hurt them.

"Tim," Glad said over the tension in the room. "You and Jake go to the kitchen and take Sis with you. Darcy, please make sure that they wash up before they get a cookie each."

Gordon didn't take his eyes off the children as not one of them moved. When Glad put her hand on the oldest child's shoulder, she whimpered. Gordon took a step back and walked right into someone.

"Don't," the voice behind him said. "They're very skittish. Would you mind very much going down to their level? I promise you they won't hurt you. At least, I don't think they will. But one never knows about the short people, do they? They can go all over the place when it comes to—"

The voice behind the papered area spoke again. This time he could hear the exasperation in her voice. "Just answer his questions then get him the hell out of my store."

He nodded before going down to his knees, ignoring the voice from beyond. "I'm Officer Force. Hello." He glanced at the person behind him then at the papered up display window.

"She won't come out until she's finished with the thingy she's doing in there anyways. I'm Justine, but everyone calls me Jessie, and these are my nieces and nephews. Children, please come and meet Officer Force." The woman got down on her knees as well. "Sis, come here and meet him. He is here on business and he—"

"I'm not going anywhere with him. You can try, but I'm not going anywhere without my sisters and brother. You can't make me." The older boy, Tim, took a stance that said, "You may be bigger, but I've learned to fight meaner." "And if you've come to tell us about our dad, you can go to hell."

Gordon didn't move. He heard the sharp intake of breath beside him, then he heard the creak of steps. Someone else had joined the fray. He nearly turned toward the noise when a younger woman stepped in front of him, one that hadn't been in the room until then.

"Timothy Allen Booth, what have I told you?" Tim's head dropped immediately. "I will not tolerate that attitude one bit and you know it. Apologize this minute," she snapped.

Gordon started to say it was all right, but the woman next to him put her hand on his arm. He glanced over at the older woman when she smiled again. This time, he could see the strain around her mouth and eyes.

"He scared Sis. Shouldn't he—?" A single step toward the boy from the standing woman had him shutting up. "I'm sorry for being rude, Officer Force. I had no...no right to be mean to you, though you scared my little sister."

5

When the hand at his arm lifted, he put out his hand. "No hard feelings. I'm sort of the same way when it comes to protecting my little sister too. I'm very sorry to have frightened her, and I apologize to you both for doing so."

The little boy looked up at the woman still standing between him and the children. With a slight nod from her, Tim walked up to Gordon and shook his hand. Tim turned to his sister and brother and nodded. "This is my sister Darcy and my sister Sis. Her real name is Abigail, but it was too hard for us to say when she was little so we called her 'Sis.' This is my brother Jake. He's not afraid of you either." Then he turned to Glad. "Can we still have the cookie? I'll make sure we clean up after ourselves."

"Of course. Come along. Maybe I'll have one for myself. I think I could easily eat a dozen right now," Glad said as she followed them out of the room. "Good heavens, how much longer is spring break anyway? I never knew it could be so nerve-wracking." Her voice faded as she went behind the curtain.

Gordon stood when the other woman did. He turned to her and noticed that the woman that had reprimanded Tim still stood watching the now empty doorway. He decided she was either very rude or very terrified for the children. He looked at the other woman before speaking. "As I was saying, I'm here to pick up some things for my family. They made me a list to bring home." He handed it to Justine. "They use the product all the time and CJ was happy when she found that you'd opened the store here in town." He was babbling. He had no idea why other than the fact that the woman still had not moved. Justine kept glancing at her too, but whoever she was remained stoic.

"There's a storm coming. Jessie, make sure Officer Force has what he needs." She turned then. "Then lock up. I have to go to the house."

Gordon felt his world slip out of sync. She was beautiful. Not only that, but drop dead, oh my fucking God, I've gone to heaven gorgeous. He started to step toward her. He needed her scent, needed, he realized, to mark her. Before he could gain control of himself, she took several steps back and turned to leave. He felt his beast snarl at him to go after her when she was just suddenly gone. He looked back at Jessie.

"My niece. She's a bit of an oddball, but what can you do?" She walked toward the shelves and started taking things off one. "She's the owner. We don't let her out from behind her cook area in the barn often, but she does pay our checks. And she makes the best eye-catching displays."

Gordon looked at the woman who was speaking, realizing that he was still staring at the now closed door. "I need to speak to her. Will she be back any time soon?"

While he couldn't exactly remember what he needed to talk to her about, he knew now that it was imperative that he did. He smelled the air and tried to find her scent, but all he could smell were soaps and herbs and the children. The children had a scent that made his wolf hum. He knew they weren't what he was, but had been with one.

"No. Not today. Well, that's not true. She'll be back sometime tonight after dark to finish the display and unveil it. When we come in tomorrow it'll be all beautiful." She put a basket of things on the counter. "Did you want everything on this list, Officer Force, or did you just want the things that were circled?"

Gordon looked at the list she was handing him and realized he didn't have a clue. Nodding, he told her to put it all in and he'd sort it out later. He looked over at the display and then the door the woman had gone out of. In no time he was out the door and almost three hundred dollars poorer. Taking out his cell, he called his brother Dallas.

"I need you to find some information for me. An address and a...." He looked back at the building. He had no idea what her name was. The paper he'd been given said GJA Incorporated, and he guessed now it was probably a combination of the names of the women. "A name. Her name will start with an 'A.'"

"I won't find you dates, Gordon. I draw the line at stalking women, even for you."

Gordon winced at his brother's words. He knew he deserved it, but still, it kind of hurt. "Nope. Not like that at all. She's supposedly a witch, and when I got here today I couldn't get much out of anyone other than she makes the displays and that she is the owner." Gordon glanced down at the two bags in his hand. "And tell CJ she owes me big time."

~~~

Alexis watched the man get into his cruiser and drive away from her stance at the side of the building of her shop. She had known it would be only a matter of time before the cops showed up. Alexis had hoped that it would have been later, but it seemed that no matter where she went someone was going to complain.

Turning back to her car, she slipped inside. Driving to the next town, she went to the store to get something for dinner, smiling when she thought of the things she'd heard about her and her family. Witches. Alexis shook her head as she answered her cell phone.

"Did you know there were wolves here when you bought this place?" her sister's husband demanded. "This could be bad for you if you did this on purpose."

"Ask me if I give a shit how this affects you." She tossed a chicken into her cart and decided to have fried chicken for dinner. Cutting the thing up could give her some much needed release. "Where's the money you said you'd send for the children? It's now seven weeks late. Again."

"You wanted them, you'll fucking keep them. For now anyway. If I find out that you've been talking to someone again, Allie, I won't hesitate to take them from you." His laughter sent a chill down her spine. "And this time I won't stop at just roughing them up a bit.'

Alexis wondered if there was any way for her to murder her own brother-in-law and get away with it. She wanted to threaten him, but knew that if she tried he'd only make good on his threat and take the kids again. She'd thought that moving there, closer to her aunts, she'd be able to protect them better, but she'd been wrong. Nearly dead wrong before, but this was home to them, to the kids and her aunts.

"Paddy, I'm only going to say this once more. You hurt those children again and, so help me, you'll pray for death when I'm finished with you." She closed her phone and looked up at the woman who was staring at her unashamedly. "Can I help you?" Alexis flushed. She hadn't meant to snap at the woman and wished now that she'd simply not answered the phone.

The woman grinned at her and held out her hand. "CJ Force. You must really have it bad for that person." Alexis shrugged at her observation. "I know what you mean. My family is like that, in that you want to murder them one minute and hug the shit out of them the next."

"You've no idea," Alexis said softly. "I'm very sorry for snapping at you like that. If you'll excuse me, I'll be on my way." She tried to push her cart around her, only just realizing that her last name was the same as the officer's.

"You're new around here, aren't you?" the woman said as she moved her cart next to Alexis's. "My husband and I just moved into the house on Blueberry Lane. Well, the entire pa...family has moved."

Every time she moved her cart to go around the woman, she'd block her again. After several attempts, Alexis realized she was doing it on purpose.

Alexis stared at her. "You're very pushy, aren't you? Has it occurred to you that I'm trying to be polite and get away from you? I have things to do, and doing social hour with you isn't really high on my list of 'gotta do today.'"

CJ threw back her head and laughed. Alexis couldn't help it, she laughed too. She'd had a shitty morning, a crappy day, and this woman wasn't going to let her get by with it. She had no idea why she immediately liked her, but took a chance and hoped she wasn't related to the cop from earlier.

"Would you like to start over? I'm CJ Force, and I'm reasonably sure you're new to this area. Would you like to get some dinner?"

"Alexis Dark, and yes to both. I'll just have to call...." Alexis remembered the cop and decided that having a cop as a friend of a friend might be too much. "I need to ask you something first. And I'm sorry if you think this is rude, but you're not by any chance related to an Officer Force, are you?" *Please say no*, her mind screamed at her.

"Yes, unfortunately, he's my brother-in-law. Did he hit on you? Which one was it? I have two in the department. Well, one will be quitting soon, but for now two. I'm betting it was Gordon. For some reason he thinks all women love him and he's...are you all right?"

No, she wasn't. A cop. She nodded then shook her head. Alexis looked at the stuff in her cart and the few things she'd put on the belt to be paid for. Should she just leave it, or pay and make her escape? She couldn't have the police around...Paddy would know. She started tossing things on the conveyor belt and then pulled out her credit card.

"I'm fine. I have to go. I just remembered that I couldn't...." Alexis took a deep breath. "I have to go, Mrs. Force. I'm sorry, but...." Handing the girl her credit card to pay, she snatched up her two bags and flew out the door.

She was nearly home before she realized that she'd left her card. Giving in to the tears that she never let fall, she pulled to the side of the road and let herself have a really good sob. It took her an extra hour to get home and, once there, she simply handed the groceries to her aunt and shook her head when she started to ask. She made her way to her rooms before she could see anyone else.

She didn't want to move again.

# CHAPTER 2

"Your new girlfriend is Alexis Dark. She's the owner of Dark Treasures in town. Mom and Holly used to buy things from her over the Internet, and now they can just go into town." Gordon nodded at his brother's information. "She and two other women, a Gladys Dark and a Justine Andrews, live out on Saddle Brook Lane. Alexis moved here about ten months ago and bought the house and about ten acres. She paid cash."

That information made the cop in him pay attention. He also decided not to tell his brother that she wasn't his anything. "How much cash, and did anyone inquire as to where the money had come from?"

"Not that I'm aware of. But I did do a little digging and found out she had a sister that died a year ago. There was a big stink over her death. Alexis claimed her brother-in-law, Patrick Booth, killed her and the authorities claimed it was a mountain lion." Dallas paused just a bit and Gordon knew he wasn't going to like the rest. "Others claim it was a wolf."

"And you know this how? Or do I want to find out?" Dallas tossed a file across the table at him and he opened it. The thing was full of pictures. Before he could ask about them, they heard a car pull into the drive.

Gordon looked up when the back door to the kitchen opened and CJ walked in. He and Dallas jumped up to take the bags and set them on the counter for her. Dallas went to the car to get the rest while Gordon started going through the bags to find himself a snack.

"I met someone who knows you today," CJ started. He grinned at her from behind. She wasn't very good at hiding her scents yet and he knew she was upset about something. "She asked me if I was related to you, then took off like I'd tried to run her down with my rig. Want to explain that one to me?"

He took the pitcher of tea from her and drew down two glasses. He took his time and tried to remember if he'd pissed anyone off lately that would talk to CJ. No one came to mind so he just shrugged.

"Nope. Must have been Connor this time. I'm innocent until you can prove otherwise." He handed her the tea. "And you owe me two hundred and ninety-four dollars and ten cents for that crap I...." He stared at her, thinking that maybe it was too small a world if Alexis had run into CJ. Either that or she was looking for him through her. He set his glass down and leaned against the counter as Dallas brought in the rest of the bags.

"What is it? Are there so many women in your harem that you have trouble keeping them all straight? Damn it, Gordon, I liked this girl. She was rude and tried to avoid me."

He frowned at CJ. "And of course you would think that is the basis for a long and lasting friendship? What the hell did she do, run right out and find you to pay me back or something?" Gordon flushed. CJ had that look about her that said he'd gone too far. He knew he shouldn't piss her off, but there were times when it was easier to go a round or two with her than one of his brothers. Sometimes anyway. He suddenly didn't think this was going to be one of those times.

"What did you do to her? I'm not kidding, Gordon Force. You'll tell me what you did to piss this girl off or so help me, I'll...I'll do something you'll regret." She was his alpha person and he knew better than to argue with her. But he was just as pissed as she seemed to be.

"What the hell do you think I am, huh? A monster? I went to her shop like *you* asked me to and, while there, I was going to clear up a few of the rumors I'd heard around town." He heard Dallas tell him to back off, but was too far gone to heed his advice. "How the fuck was I to know she was going to be all pissy about me talking to the kids? I didn't do a damn thing to them other than to fucking say hi."

"That's enough," the voice thundered behind him. Gordon didn't even have to turn to know that his brother and alpha was standing right behind him. He closed his eyes and then opened them as he turned.

"Don't, Austin," CJ told him. "He and I were just talking. And I started it. I was wrong and I shouldn't have jumped on him like that." She hugged him before going to her mate. "He didn't do anything to upset me, and I flew off the handle before I thought about it."

"He should know better than to snap at you. He and I will talk about this later." Gordon snorted at Austin. "You think this is a joke? She's whelping, you shit head, and I'll have you take a care."

The low growl had them both step back. Even though CJ hadn't been a wolf long, she was still an alpha. Gordon took another step back from her when she snarled at Austin.

"Honey, you—"

"You say one word, you overgrown dog, and I will rip your nuts off your body and serve them up at the next pack meeting. How do you expect me to be the alpha person if you are always stepping in and taking over? Back the fuck up right fucking now." Austin glared at Dallas when he laughed. "Don't think that because I'm pissed at him right now that you're off the hook either, smart boy."

Gordon watched as she turned on Dallas. Since he was grinning when she turned to him, she caught him as well. "CJ, I'm sorry. Why don't you tell me who you met and I'll try to tell you how I pissed her off."

Being the brother-in-law to an alpha person had its advantages. Mostly, it was having her around to calm his brother, but there were times when he simply liked to tease her. And he had to laugh every time she glared at him. To himself, though.

Gordon knew who it was that she was talking about, but it didn't hurt to have a little confirmation just to be sure. When CJ started digging through her purse, he thought maybe it was someone else until she turned and looked at him with a smile. When she handed him a credit card with Alexis D. Dark on it, he simply sat down.

Dallas looked at the card and then sat down beside him. "This the same girl, I take it? The one you had me looking for this morning?"

Gordon nodded. "Yeah. She left her shop and ran into CJ, I guess. I'm guessing that it was a chance meeting and nothing prearranged."

CJ nodded at him. "She was in a bad mood when I first saw her. She was talking to somebody on the phone. And since I have the hearing of a bat now I heard the man threaten her about some children, and she told him that she'd make him pay if he touched them again. I don't think I'd want to piss her off if I could avoid it. She looks like she'd be vicious."

Gordon took the file again and looked at the pictures inside. He pulled out the ones of the kids. They were smiling in the picture in his hand, much different than the look they'd had in the store. There they'd looked haunted rather than happy like they seemed with the woman beside them.

"I met these kids today. Though they are not the same now as they were then…they've been hurt and hurt badly. This one, Timothy." He pointed at the oldest boy. "He was ready to take me on to save his family. He thought I was there to take him away. And he didn't want anything to do with his father."

"So something happened to them? And you're thinking their father is involved?" CJ sat down and picked up the file as she spoke. She was about halfway through it when she set it down again. "I can't look at those anymore. They're…you have to make sure they're all safe, Gordon. You can't let that man, whoever he is, harm them."

He knew that, but didn't know what he was up against. The scent on the kids had made him think that there was another wolf around. He looked at the pictures and then thought about the scent. Male was all he'd really gotten and that somehow he'd been around the children recently. He'd bet his last dollar that the woman, Alexis, didn't know it either.

He held the credit card in his hand and looked over at Austin. "There was a wolf around the kids recently. I'm not sure who, but it wasn't anyone familiar to me, not pack anyway. At first I thought that it was one of the adults, but I don't think any of them are were. Do you suppose that this man really did kill the other girl and he's a wolf too?"

"He'd be in violation of pack law if he's in the area without informing me. If this Dark woman is harboring him, which I highly doubt, then she could be in just as much trouble as him." Austin took the file from in front of CJ. He studied it for several minutes before he, too, closed the file and set it back down. "These are wolf marks, but not all of them. Some are from a knife, very sharp, and steel. Anyone who knows a wolf would be able to tell that."

Gordon only nodded. The woman had been murdered, there was no doubt about that, but by a wolf he wasn't so sure. The attack had been violent and brutal. The marks on the woman's throat and belly were extensive and were more than likely what had killed her. She'd been torn apart and eviscerated as well, her intestines torn from her and spilled onto the ground. Whoever had done this to her had been there to do just what they'd done…kill, and kill for the sport of it.

Gordon stood up and kissed CJ on the cheek just to hear his brother growl. Smiling, he turned to his brother Dallas and held out the file. He wanted some answers, and he figured he'd get them best at the house rather than the shop.

"I'm going to go and see our Miss Dark. I think it's time we had a little chat about customer service and politeness to others." He grinned when he looked up at CJ. "Want to come with me?"

"No, I do not. But I will give you advice, a woman thing." She grinned at him when he frowned at her. He so didn't need advice about women. "Don't do like you normally do with woman."

He pretended to frown at her harder. "You mean don't be my usual charming self? CJ, you wound me. Women love me. I have them eating out of my hands all the time."

"This one doesn't strike me as the 'Gordon notch in the bedpost' sort of woman, and I'm pretty sure she can take you." Then she punched him slightly in the shoulder. "And if you play your cards right I might get a discount at the shop, and that'll go a long way in making me love you more."

Gordon was still laughing at her when he went out the door. Women loved him and he was sure he could get this one to love him too…or at least like him a bit. She'd been having a bad day, that was all, and he'd simply woo her to his way of thinking while he got a little information.

~~~

The knock at her door made her groan. She didn't move from the soapy bath, but closed her eyes against the noise. She tried to concentrate on the sounds her headphones were pumping into her ears, but the pounding was getting on her last nerve. Alexis stepped out of the tub, grabbed a towel, and went to give the person on the other side a piece of her mind and the feel of her fist. She jerked back when she saw who was standing there.

"Your aunt said I could come down. She thought maybe you were asleep and told me to…. Do you have anything on under that towel?"

"Of course I do. Don't you take a bath fully clothed?" Alexis wanted to turn and find more to put on, but was sure it was too late for that. "What the hell do you want, Officer Force? I'm on my own time here and you're interrupting my down time."

"I can see that." She would bet he was seeing a great deal. "I wanted to talk to you about something. Something important. Something…. Don't you want to get something less…more on? I mean, I'm sure you have to have a robe or something back there." He looked over her shoulder like one was suddenly going to appear for her.

"I do, and to put it on would waste more of my time since I'm going to strip down and get back into my bath as soon as you leave." She glanced back to the clock at the side of her bed. "In about five seconds."

She shouldn't have looked away. Looking away gave him enough time to move and, when he had, he'd taken full advantage of the open door. Suddenly, he was standing right in front of her, and he smelled so good. She was nearly ready to lean into him and smell his neck when he touched her.

"Do you have any idea how lovely you are?" He skimmed his finger along the swell of her breasts that the towel was pressing over. "And your skin is very warm, almost hot. I'm betting you smell very good too. Can I have a sniff of you, Miss Dark? A taste maybe?"

She closed her eyes to the almost purr of his voice. It was hypnotic and the most soothing thing she'd ever heard in her life. When she found herself pressed against him, she looked up into his eyes, suddenly very afraid and very needy.

"Don't," she said as he lowered his head to hers. "Please, don't."

"Too late." He brushed his mouth over hers once then pulled back to look at her again. "Christ, it's you." This time when he took her mouth it was to devour her.

His hand at her breast made her breath catch even as his tongue invaded her mouth. And when she felt him moan her pussy tightened then moistened. She shifted on her feet as she lifted her hand to his hair and laced her fingers in its softness. Moaning again when his mouth moved down her neck to her shoulder, she could almost hear the pounding of her heart, it was so loud. When his mouth took her nipple, she nearly came apart. This time when she begged him it was for an entirely different reason.

"I want you. Right now. I want to taste your sweetness and then come inside of you," Gordon whispered in her ear as he made his way up her throat again. "Tell me you want me as well, Alexis. Tell me that you need me too."

*Yes,* her mind screamed at her. *Tell him yes.* But before she could form the words he was nipping at her neck, and the sudden pain that flared through her was gone before she could protest.

"Please, you're going too fast," she tried. "I need to—"

"Mine," he told her as he slid his finger deep inside of her pussy. "Come for me. Come while I make you mine."

His tongue laved her throat again and she was melting against him when he pinched her clit. As she cried out, her climax moved over her entire body, and when she felt him sink his teeth hard into the flesh of the pulse of her throat she knew she was a goner. The second climax took her breath away, and she felt the world darken around her.

When she opened her eyes she was on her bed. Sitting up, she found that her towel was laid over her and she was alone in the room. She might have thought it was all a dream, but her neck ached where he'd bitten her and she could see a red mark on her breast where he'd suckled at her nipple. Angry at both him and herself, she stood and nearly toppled over when a wave of dizziness rolled over her. She couldn't stand at first and had to hold onto the bed until it passed.

Making her way to her bathroom, Alexis was cussing the fucking man. What for, she wasn't sure. It was either that he'd left her after those incredible climaxes or that he'd given them to her in the first place. Either way, he was a dead man if he came around again. She didn't need any more arrogant, pushy men in her life. One was more than she could handle right now.

Pulling on the first thing she could find, she was out of the bedroom and on her way to the barn before she could think. Well, she did think, but she wasn't happy about where her thoughts were taking her. Men, knives, and blood were running rapt with sex, silky sheets, and screaming climaxes.

She was in her lab later that night when she heard the kids coming across the lot. She had to smile at them. They were a handful, but she loved them dearly. How could she not? They were her sister's children and she missed her more with every passing day. And the children had suffered much worse than her. Especially Darcy.

Darcy hadn't spoken a word since the day the police had found her covered in blood and hiding in the barn. Alexis had taken her there when she'd run from the house to find the man—the men in this case—who had killed her mother. She'd only meant to protect the girl, but they all had thought that she'd gone there after witnessing the murder.

The doctors had told Alexis that Darcy had probably seen the killing of her mother and was still in shock. But Alexis knew better. She knew for a fact that she'd seen her mother killed and also the person who had done it. It had been a shock for her as well to know that a man could kill his own wife and do it in front of his children. But Paddy hadn't been alone, nor had he been the one to give her sister the final blow that ended her life.

Alexis had wanted to hit the doctors for their astute observations. She worked with her niece every day to try and get her to at least say something, anything that told her that she was going to be all right. The children crashing open the door had her racing to the front part of the work area.

"He's here," Tim said with his eyes wide. "He's comed for us and I'm not going back with him."

"Go. Now." She herded them to the underground levels that she'd had specially made for them. She'd no more than thrown the rug back over the opening when Paddy Booth came in the building.

"Where the fuck are they? I know that you're hiding them and I want them right fucking no—" He stopped speaking suddenly and sniffed the air. "What the hell have you done?"

His fist hit her so quickly that she barely had time to see it coming, much less duck out of its way. She knew she needed to stay alert or he'd kill her. But at some point she couldn't stay awake any longer.

# CHAPTER 3

Austin went into the kitchen. His mother had come in his office a few minutes earlier and said that Gordon was there and he looked pole axed. She thought something had happened, but since he was still staring off into space she couldn't get a word out of him.

"I think that girl did something to him. It's rumored she's a witch. Maybe she put a hex on him or something." Nancy Force grinned. "But I'm thinking it might be something altogether different."

"Gordon?" His brother looked up at him. "Mom said that you were—"

"I didn't mean to do it. I just…she was only wearing this towel, and when I touched her, it was everything I could do not to throw her to the floor and take her."

Austin sat down, his knees already a little shaky from seeing his brother look so pale and distraught. He wasn't sure what his brother was talking about, but his mom was right, something had happened. He just hoped that Gordon hadn't hurt anyone in his rough housing.

"Who? Are you talking about the girl? The one from this morning? Tell me what happened. I'm sure that whatever it is, we can figure out something." At least he hoped so.

"I just wanted to kiss her...well, I wanted her, and once I touched her I couldn't stop. Then I realized who she was and it was too late. You think maybe it was a mistake?" Gordon started nodding his head. "Yeah, that's it. I just didn't get it right. No way could that be right."

"Christ. Please tell me you didn't rape the girl. So help me, Gordon, if you did, there won't be a place deep enough for you to hide in that I won't find you." He got up and started to pace when he suddenly got a scent from his brother. "Mother fuck. You've mated."

"What the fuck do you think I've been trying to tell you? I told you, I only meant to kiss her, and then I realized as soon as I touched her who she was. Or thought I did. You think it was a mistake?"

Austin sat down again, hard. "No. I think you've met your mate and that you've at least partially mated with her. Christ, love a duck. What does she say about all this? I'm sure she's just thrilled to no end."

"I didn't tell her. After she climaxed...twice...I picked her up, put her on the bed, and got the hell out of there. Maybe she won't notice. Maybe...ah hell, Austin, what the hell am I going to do with a mate?"

"Whose mate? You aren't screwing around with another wolf...." Dallas burst out laughing after he leaned down and took a big whiff of Gordon's shirt. "You've met her, I see. The girl from this morning? She's a looker. I wouldn't mind if I had—"

Dallas was suddenly across the room on the floor and Gordon was over him with his arm at his brother's throat.

It had happened so fast that Austin barely had time to get out of the way before he was caught in the fray.

"Stay away from my mate." The threat was delivered with a low and blood-chilling tone. "She's mine."

None of them moved, especially not Dallas. He should have known better than to say anything like that to a mated wolf, even in jest. Austin walked slowly over to both men and kneeled down to look at Gordon.

"Let him up," he told him with as much compulsion as he could. "Tell him you're sorry, Dallas, and then, Gordon, I want you to let him up."

He watched as Gordon started to relax. It was a few more tense seconds before he stood, and then he offered Dallas his hand. Austin was afraid he wasn't going to take it. Dallas just stared at Gordon. Then when he spoke Austin was sure this wasn't the end of it.

"You know me better than to think I'd touch your mate, I would hope." Dallas finally took his hand and stood. "Next time you have a beef with me, I suggest you be more polite about it or I'll kick your ass."

They sat at the table, but not before Gordon got them each a beer. The tension around the table chilled a bit, but it wasn't until Gordon started talking that things got better.

"She was supposed to be sleeping, her aunt said. She told me to go on down and wake her up and for us both to come up for dinner. How the hell was I supposed to know she'd answer the door half naked and smelling like sex? Christ," he said as he took a long pull from his bottle. "She is beautiful. Dark hair that was curling up like it was going to be messy in no time. Eyes the color of the night sky in the middle of summer when all the street lights are out. And Christ, what a body. It was everything I could do not to take more than I did from her."

"You bit her then?" Dallas asked. "You didn't waste any time, did you? I mean, what did you do, meet her this morning and mate with her tonight?"

"It was like I couldn't help myself. As soon as I tasted her skin, tasted her mouth, I knew that it wasn't going to be enough." Gordon looked down at his beer as he continued. "She's going to be pissed, isn't she? I mean, I didn't hurt her, not really, and I did make it feel good for her too."

Austin looked up when his mate came in the room with his mom. He knew that she had heard his brother's last statement the moment she walked in the room. Austin wanted to feel sorry for his brother, but he was completely on his own with this one. Taking a mate was hard enough, but taking a human one was really scary. Austin looked over at CJ and then pulled her into his lap when she got close enough for him to touch.

There was a good deal to be happy about in taking a mate too. This, as he snuggled into her neck, was the best part. Then he laid his hand over her growing little mound that was their child. He smiled when she grinned at him.

"When are you going to bring her around, Gordon? Your mom will love her, by the way. I already do. Having another female in this family will be really nice too. We can go shopping and do lunch together."

Gordon flushed before answering. "I have to tell her what she is to me first. It's going to be bad, and then there are the kids. I'm not sure what they are to her, but they're pretty scared of people."

"You'll have to tell her very soon. If there is another wolf in her family and he finds out, things could be bad for her. Or the kids," Dallas said as he poured CJ a glass of milk and their mom a glass of tea. "I've been trying to find out what I can about the brother-in-law, but all I've found so far is that he and the sister, Judith Dark Booth, had been divorced about two years before the murder. He'd been accused of being into some drugs and some thefts, but now...it's as if he just dropped off the face of the earth."

Gordon's phone ringing startled them all and then the pack phone going off sent them all off. Dallas snatched up the pack phone just as Gordon started writing down things in his notebook. He stood as soon as he closed his phone.

"I have to go. A woman was just brought into the hospital by her family. They say she's been beat up pretty badly. I'm on call so—"

"It's Alexis Dark," Dallas said. "Carol at the hospital called to tell me that she has been beaten by a wolf. His scent is all over her. He...Christ, she said he beat her pretty bad."

Gordon was out the door and into his car before the rest of them could gather coats and purses. Dallas went out with him and Austin went with the women. Connor, their brother, showed up just as they were loading into the car, and he jumped in with them. Austin hoped it wasn't as bad as they said, but he had a feeling that it was going to be much worse.

~~~

Alexis could only open one eye and it was blurry. She tried to roll over, but it hurt too badly so she simply moved her head. That wasn't much better, but at least she could see more. The first person she saw was the cop from earlier.

"The call came in and I'm on duty. How are you feeling?" he asked as he put his face down to her level. "They are going to give you something for pain, but the doc said he wanted to assess your pain level first."

"Ten times infinity," she told him as she tried to move again. "The kids? Where are they?"

"In the lobby with my mom and your aunt. Tim is trying to decide if he trusts us or not, and Sis is telling my mom all about her dad." He brushed the hair from her mouth as he continued. "He sounds like a real winner. Did he hit you?"

She didn't even try to pretend she was going to answer him. Alexis had enough going on at the moment, and a nosey cop in the mix wasn't going to help her. Especially not with Paddy and the children, and most assuredly with all the other shit she was trying to juggle.

"I'd like for you to go away, please. I don't know who called the cops, but nothing is the matter. I...I fell, that's all." She hated lying, but whatever had pissed off Paddy, she was sure he wasn't finished with her yet. "I'm really okay. Thanks anyway."

She tried to get him to back off by sitting up, but he just pressed her back into the bed. When she tried it a second time, he leaned down to her and nipped at her ear lobe. Her body seemed to like it a whole lot more than she thought it should. When he licked her pulse, she couldn't help but moan.

"Unless you want me to join you in this bed to keep you here, I would suggest you be still." Her body shivered in reaction to his threat. "Christ, you smell delicious."

His mouth moved along her throat and then along her ear again. She could feel him with her entire body. Feel everything about this man and what he was doing to her. She moaned when he moved to cup her breast. She was about to beg him, for what she wasn't sure, but he suddenly stiffened and she moaned again when he didn't continue.

"Gordon," someone said from behind him. When he started to pull away, she whimpered. The damned man actually winked at her after he kissed her quickly.

"Alexis, this is my brother Austin, and you've met his lovely wife CJ." The door opened again and another man walked in with a pretty older woman. "This is one of my other brothers, Dallas, and my mom, Nancy."

Alexis nodded. She was too busy trying to get her hand from Gordon to pay much attention to what was going on. Plus, she hurt. Her head was pounding and her busted lip felt heavy and swollen. Every time she moved she could feel where Paddy had kicked her...even her toes hurt to wiggle them. When she was finally able to free herself, she huffed when he sat on the edge of her bed and put his hand on her leg.

"Miss Dark, could you tell us what happened today? Who hit you—?"

She cut off the one he'd called Dallas. "No one hit me. As I've told this man, I fell. Not that it's any of your business anyway. So I'd very much like it if you all left."

CJ giggled and Alexis wasn't sure, but she thought the mother laughed as well before Dallas glared at her. With a raised brow, Mrs. Force had him backing off. That too might have been funny, but Alexis had had enough. She finally managed to press the nurse's call button before anyone else could ask her about today. The nurse answered and Alexis asked for a doctor.

"Miss Dark…Alexis…there's no reason for you to try and protect your brother-in-law. We take care of our own whether it be the victim or the abuser." She laughed at Dallas's statement as he continued. "We have laws…laws that are enforced to keep everyone safe. Especially when our females are hurt."

The nurse coming in the room kept her from telling him just what he could do with his laws of safety. Ignoring all of them, but especially the one trying to grab for her hand again, she simply smiled at the nurse.

"Doctor Cable is on his way up, miss," Nurse Jenny said while she glanced around the room nervously. "He's not going to be happy about all the visitors either. It's not even visiting hours. And that man is a stickler for rules."

"Exactly," Alexis snapped before turning to Gordon with a final jerk of her hand from his. "What is with you? I want you to stop touching me. In fact, why don't you and the rest of your family get the hell out?"

She tried to move away from him again. Then he did something that made her blood freeze and her heart skip several beats. He growled low in the back of his throat. Terror slammed at her. She managed to look him in the eye as she asked what she thought she might already know. "What…what are you?" she whispered. And she knew…just knew that he was going to tell her something she didn't want to know.

"I'm a wolf. A born werewolf, as a matter of fact. Not like your brother-in-law, but one born to parents who were weres." He leaned closer to her and her nipples peaked even though she was terrified. "And I'm your mate."

# CHAPTER 4

Gordon waited until the doctor left her room before he went to the door again. The past three times he'd tried to see her someone, usually her Aunt Glad, was blocking his path. He could have moved her out of his way, but Alexis was upset enough without him physically moving her aunt so that he could explain. And this time wasn't any different.

"You could have handled that a little better."

Gordon leaned back against the wall near Alexis's door before he answered his mom. "I know. I should have guessed she'd been hurt more than just today by him." Gordon glanced over at the kids. "If she's that terrified of him, I wonder what he's done to those guys."

Tim kept giving him that look, the one that said, "I'm watching you." The little girl, Sis, would talk your arm off, but even with the little time he'd spent with her, he could tell she was afraid. She also kept reaching for someone's hand to hold as if she was terrified of being left behind. Jake wasn't a typical kid…quiet and reserved, but friendly when he spoke. It was Darcy who he was worried about the most. She'd been hurt, and hurt badly.

She didn't speak, at least not since they'd come in with the aunts. She simply sat next to Glad and stared at the floor. When someone spoke to her she would look toward them, but she never made eye contact, nor did she acknowledge anyone in any way. He would bet his last dollar that the father had done something to her, or she'd seen him do something that had terrified her.

"What are you going to do?" his mom asked, bringing his mind away from whatever Darcy's father may have done. "I'm sure I don't have to remind you that she's your mate, Gordon. You need her."

He nodded. "But I don't know what happened, so I can't show her I won't hurt her." He looked over at the kids. "Or the kids. And I think that alone will keep her from trusting me."

The door opened beside them and Alexis came out in a wheel chair. He knew she'd been released AMA, or against medical advice, and he wondered if she'd be all right. He didn't say anything to her, but followed behind her, the nurse, and Jessie. He waited until they were outside before he knelt down in front of her. Speaking softly, he looked at her.

"I won't hurt you. Not ever. It's in my DNA to never be able to harm you or your family." Not unless they harmed her, he thought, but didn't share that with her. "Friday was going to be my last day on the job, but under the circumstances, the boss is letting me—"

"He knows what you are? What you're capable of?"

He'd expected this from her, but it still hurt him that she would have so low an opinion of him. "Yes, he knows I'm a werewolf. He also knows I can be trusted." She

36

snorted, but he continued. "I won't hurt you, Alexis. I know this is a lot to take in, but after a little bit of time, you'll be—"

"No, I won't. You'll need to stay away from me and the children, Officer Force. I want nothing to do with you. I have enough going on right now and I don't want you coming around messing things up for me and the children." He heard the car pull up behind him as she continued. "Now if you don't mind, I need to get home."

When she stood, so did he. He was hurt and pissed off or he might have been a little gentler with her. But he wanted her, right now. He wanted her with all his being. Pulling her to him, he took her mouth. When she whimpered a little, he pulled back, but didn't let her go. Cupping her ass in his hand, he rocked her into him, letting her feel just what she did to him.

His cock ached to be free and buried deep inside of her. Moving down her jaw with his lips, he tasted her blood again, this time from her cut lip. The sweetness of it from when he'd bitten her earlier came rushing back to him. Need coiled in his belly and groin and had his wolf snarling at him to claim her.

She tangled her fingers into his hair and he pulled her tighter. With his mouth he worked his way down her throat to his mark. The need to bite her again almost as overwhelming as the need to mate with her, he felt her shift and then there was pain. It was slowly making him aware of his balls and that she'd kicked him. It blossomed in his lower belly and then out to every part of him. He could almost feel it in his hair follicles.

As he dropped to his knees he heard someone behind him say, "fuck." It might have been any one of his brothers...he just didn't care. He curled into a ball just as the car was pulling away. He watched it from the level of the sidewalk, wondering if he could get it to come back and run over him at least once to take away the pain.

He decided he was going to have to make her pay for this. He could think of one or two ways right off the top of his head he was going to enjoy. Spanking her tight little ass sounded very good right now.

"Hurts, huh?" Gordon glanced at his brother Connor who had just spoken. "Women just don't play fair when they knee you like that. I wonder who the first man was they did that to and how he reacted." Connor looked out across the lot before he spoke again. "Mom and CJ went to get the car for you. Austin and Dallas are over there still laughing at you."

Gordon could hear them now. The pain was receding enough that he could think around it. He decided they were going to pay as well. It just wouldn't be as pleasurable as the plans he had for Alexis and him.

He groaned as he sat up. "I did this, not her. I should have been a lot better about this. I didn't explain things well enough and now she's scared." He hoped that he'd have the opportunity to make things right.

Connor was nodding before he finished speaking. He looked off to where their brothers were talking to CJ when Connor spoke again. This time his voice was hard.

"I think I might have met the one that hurt her. Well, not met him per se, but I have seen his dirty work. I could smell him on her." Connor leaned back and took something out of his pocket. "This is the notice that I got from one of the guys I work with. He doesn't know what we are, but he gave this to me to invite me to it."

Gordon took the sheet of paper and started to read it. He was about halfway through it when Dallas and Austin came up beside him. Without saying a word, he handed it up to them then stood. He waited for them to finish.

"Where did you get this?" Austin asked as he flipped the sheet over. "This has to be a joke. Why on earth would you put something out like this for real?"

It was an open invitation to come see a wolf fight. And not just any normal wolves either. It said that a werewolf was going to take on anyone that cared to step into the ring with him. There was a picture of a wolf standing over the body of a man who'd had his throat ripped out. The wolf was covered in blood and his fangs still dripped with it.

"This guy I work with gave it to me. He'd been handing them out for about an hour at the beginning of the shift, and I didn't get to see what it was until later." Gordon looked at Austin before he shuddered. "The guy in the picture, he was there too, only he was in the parking lot. I could smell him, smell his wolf. His scent was on the woman just now."

Connor was a detective now, homicide. He'd worked his way up the ranks and had taken on extra classes and jobs to be one, and in less than three years he'd finally made detective first grade. He was the best of the best in detective work. Gordon was very proud of his twin and wished him the best of luck. Gordon, however, was very content to be the second in the pack just under his brother Dallas.

"This is against our pack law. I wonder who he thinks he is just...." Austin looked at both of them. "Have either of you been to one of these? Maybe not this one, but ones like this?"

They both shook their heads, but Gordon spoke up. "I've been clean up on them though. There was a ring of these fights about six months ago and there were several men killed. They simply left the bodies behind when they moved on."

Connor nodded. "Yeah, I remember that. Seven dead with two of them wolves. They were cubs, not much older than seventeen. I couldn't say much because of the other department in charge, but the wolves had more than likely been in over their heads and had shifted back after they'd been killed."

Austin handed the paper back to Connor. "Find out what you can and be quiet about it. I don't need to tell you if the humans get wind of this they'll hunt us down. Gordon, take care of your mate. And find out if she knows anything about this and if not, then she'll need more protection."

The ride back to the pack house was noisy. They had a plan in the works before they pulled into the driveway. And when they saw Phil there sitting on the porch, they got his help as well.

~~~

Alexis looked at her face in the mirror. She looked like she'd gone a few rounds with a champ and had come out a loser. In addition to her split lip and black eye, she had several cracked ribs and the color of her torso was vivid. She pulled her shirt back down over the worst of them when she went to answer the door to her bedroom. She was surprised to see Phil there. She wasn't, though, to see Gordon with him.

"You've been busy, I see. I don't suppose I could persuade you to take me to your office to talk? I love the view from that room." She let Phil kiss her cheek and ignored the growl from the idiot behind him.

"Sure, but just so you know, if whatever you want involves him, it's a no." She led the way to her office. She, too, loved the view. "The windows were put in last week and the floors are all finished too. You should see my bedroom. Oh Phil, it's perfect."

"He will not be going to your bedroom. I don't care how nice the view is. Do you hear me, Phil? I'm serious." Alexis huffed at Gordon, but didn't comment. "I'm not kidding, Alexis. Wolves are a very jealous bunch and he'll stay out—"

"If I want to take him down there and fuck his brains out, it'll be none of your fucking business." She heard Phil tell her to stop, but she'd had enough. "What business is it of yours—?"

She was suddenly against the wall with Gordon pressing against her. He was different, and it took her several seconds to realize what it was. His eyes had changed. They were a light brown, but now there were dark, almost black, and he smelled different. He smelled.... She leaned her face into his neck and sniffed. Every nerve in her body woke up at the scent. His low growl only made her want more, more of something only he could give her, she was sure.

"Christ," she heard Phil say from behind them. "You're making me crazy over here. Mate with her later. Right now, we need to speak to her. Your scent is driving me over the edge."

Breathing hard, she looked up at Gordon again. His eyes were now the normal shade of brown, but his smell made her dizzy. She swallowed hard when he looked down at her mouth.

"He's right. We need to talk to you. But you should know that I can smell you too." He leaned down and whispered in her ear. "I can smell your arousal. Are you wet, baby?"

She wanted to tell him that the sound of his voice had made her that way since yesterday. The climaxes that he'd given her a few days ago seemed to have made her a walking nymphomaniac, and he was her only cure. She stood against the wall when he stepped back. She was afraid to look at him, so she looked at Phil.

"You need to talk to me about what? And as a lawyer, why are...? Please tell me that you're not here to tell me he's won custody of the children. Oh Phil, you assured me that he didn't have a snowball's chance in hell for—"

"No, no that's not it. We're here to...to explain. You need to be aware of what I am and what.... Perhaps you should have a seat." Phil glared at Gordon before he continued. "You know, this is the second time I've had to do this for your family to take the heat off one of you. I don't think this is such a good idea."

"But you'll help. CJ said you really helped her when she needed it, and she did tell you she really likes her. Come on, Phil, please?"

Alexis was about to remind them that she was in the room with them when Phil suddenly turned to her.

"You need to have a seat. And what I'm going to tell you is very…dangerous. Not only to me, but to you as well. Understand?"

She started to nod, then shook her head as she sat down. "No, I don't. You come in here wanting to see the view in my office and…shit, you were getting me alone. Oh no, something's happened. What is it? Is it your mom?"

"Okay." Phil sat on the floor in front of her. "You know he's a were, correct? And what that means to you?"

"I know that he did something to me that made Pa…made someone pissed off at me. What did he do, Phil? Please tell me the truth and I'll believe you."

"Oh, honey, I hope you're right. I've really come to enjoy you and your family." Phil turned and glared at Gordon, then looked back at her. "He's your mate. And as I'm aware he didn't tell you this before he marked you. I'll explain."

"Marked me? I don't…he bit me." She stood and nearly knocked Phil over. "You son of a bitch. What the fuck gave you the right to—?"

"Sit the fuck down," Phil thundered, and she sat. She was really glad she was near a couch or she might have ended up on the floor. "Now, we are going to do this like adults without name calling and certainly not with anger."

When Gordon came and sat next to her she tried to scoot away from him, but he kept moving over. With a low growl from Phil, which surprised her to no end, she sat still. Something was going on here and she wasn't all that thrilled about finding out what.

"Now, as I was saying. He marked you. Yes, I agree that he should have spoken to you before he bit you, but that is over with. He's your mate for better or worse." He glared when Gordon started to speak. "I'm doing this my way, wolf, or I walk. Your family is not on my best buddy list right now, so I suggest you shut up as well."

"Well, why don't you get to the point already? There are things going on that you're well aware of, and I can't be responsible for how she reacts later." Gordon started to stand, but waited for some approval from Phil before he started pacing. "There are things going on, things that could come to hurt you, and Phil has agreed to help me keep you safe."

She looked at them again. *Seriously*? Phil was a nice man and all, but protect her from Paddy? She didn't think he had a violent bone in his entire body. She grinned at him when he sat next to her.

"What do you suppose you can do that I can't? No offense, but you're not really the type of man I'd call if I had a bully. You're more the…behind the desk and sue their ass sort of bully." She took his hand as she continued. "I think the world of you and your family, but I think you might want to sit this one out."

"Honey," he told her with a grin that was not at all nice. "I'm more scary than anything in this room. I'm a vampire."

# CHAPTER 5

Phil waited for her to say something. He could see that she really didn't believe him. He didn't blame her. There were days when he didn't believe it himself. He sat back and waited for the questions, hysterics…something. What he got was a complete surprise.

"Vampire. Okay, so if there are werewolves, there should be something…someone bigger, right?" Alexis got up to pace as she talked seemingly to herself. "Paddy wasn't nice before he did whatever, and now he's…well, I was going to say monster, but I don't want to be mean to that species either."

"Alexis," Gordon started, only to be ignored. When he looked at him, Phil simply shook his head. He thought she might be able to work this one out on her own.

"You can walk during the day. Is that the norm for your…what are you, a species or a race?"

Phil grinned. "Race. Species makes us sound like we were invented in a lab somewhere. We're real. And no, it's not normal for a vampire to walk in the daylight hours. My mother is a pureblood and my father isn't. I can eat food as well as drink from a person. Part of my natural charm, I suppose you could say. Are you all right, honey?"

She nodded as she continued pacing and speaking. "So there are more of you. Okay. Probably lots of people I know are...aren't what they seem. I guess I'll have to pay more...CJ? Is she a...what did you call it, a were?"

"Yes," Gordon said. "CJ was turned when she mated to Austin. She's a white wolf, rare for us even as a natural wolf. She's a gift to our pack."

"Doesn't that make it hard for her to hunt?" Before either man could answer, she answered her own question. "Of course, I suppose it doesn't matter if you can just go down to the local meat market and pick up your meal. Sorry," she said flushing. "I'm trying to absorb this."

"You're doing great. Go on, work it out, love." She glared at Gordon and had Phil nearly laugh out loud from her expression.

"You'd do well to take the vampire's advice and shut up." She paced some more before she suddenly stopped and took several deep breaths. "I just told a werewolf to take the advice of a vampire and shut up. Ohmygod, ohmygod, ohmygod. I need to...I need to take.... I'll be— you'll have to—I'll be right back."

Neither man moved when she suddenly dashed out the side door to her office. She was running across the field and toward the waterfall before either man stood. When Gordon started to go after her, Phil stopped him.

"She needs this. Let her go. You've taken her blood so if she gets into trouble, you'll know it." Phil looked around the room. "You should see if there is anything in here that you can get a clue about your mate."

"What do you mean? Snoop?" Gordon shook his head. "I can't do that to her. She already doesn't trust me not to hurt her. If she figures out that I've gone through her things it'll make matters worse."

Phil looked around the room that was so much a part of the girl outside that he could see why she loved it here. He sighed heavily. He'd been a vampire for nearly four hundred years and still couldn't understand the human psyche. Even this wolf seemed to have no clue about women. Not that he was having any luck with his own mate, but that was another story.

"What do you see in this room? Take away the fact that you're a cop and look at this room as if you're looking through her eyes." Phil did the same. "The windows, the sheer size of them, what does that tell you?'

Phil looked out the large wall of windows. They'd been specially made for this room, he knew. There were three of them and they didn't just come together as much as they blended to give the room the natural setting. He didn't doubt that the woman who designed this room was as in love with nature as the man she'd been fated to be mated to.

The first window was nearly ten feet at its widest width. At the top it was about four feet and then got larger as it went to the floor. The trim around it was an old oak log. The wood had been cut in a way that the glass looked like it was there naturally. The next pane of glass was nearly fifteen feet in width. It was only a few feet smaller at the top, and it too fit into a log of dark cherry. Phil could actually smell the wood now that he was in here. The last panel of glass was over thirty feet and overlapped the next wall, which was stone from the mountain the house rested against. The masonry work alone to put the wall together had cost Alexis a fortune, but she could well afford it.

"She likes the outdoors. She has a lot of it in here as well as outside." Gordon was looking at the room from the window. "She said her bedroom had a view. The one time I was there, I don't...she and I got distracted and I can't remember what it looked like."

"Yes. When the house was being renovated I was onsite. Her room, the master suite, is below us. Much more below us. She cannot only see what's behind you, but more. Most of the room's view is of the waterfalls, and the stream goes right past her windows. When she purchased this house, she did it because of the way it sat. The builders told her that she'd never get what she had in the house, but she told them to...well, they built it to her specs, but made fun of her ideas while they did it. I think once the house was finished they were the ones eating crow."

Gordon nodded. "She spends a lot of time in here. So do the children. She has a lot of wood worked into the room. Almost as if she was trying to keep the world that's just out there at her fingertips. She...she's going to be a beautiful wolf."

Phil thought so too. Not only did he think she would be a more beautiful wolf than CJ, but he thought she'd be a bigger gift to the pack now forming. Something about Alexis made him think she wasn't simply a woman with a great deal of brains. He'd bet anything she was a woman with a little magic too.

Gordon spoke and brought him from his musings. "She doesn't trust me. Not at all, and I'm not sure what to do about that. She's been hurt, hurt more than what the other wolf did to her the other day, hasn't she? And more than…more than her sister's death. What happened, do you know?"

He did, but he didn't feel it was his story to tell. He also knew that the little girl, Darcy, was hiding behind more than her not speaking. The little girl was suffering in ways that no one could really see. He just hoped that someone reached her before it was too late.

"I can't tell you that. That tale is going to have to come from her." Phil saw her coming across the field. "Gordon, you know that she took this all very well, but I doubt that it will help you overly much in what you want from her. You should simply mate with her and then try to make her understand what you're trying to do."

Phil winced when he thought about the advice he was giving the wolf. His own mate, Gordon's sister, was driving him crazy right now. And if he could just get her in a room for more than five minutes without her taking a strip off his hide he'd do the same thing and take her. She was his mate and damn it, he was tired of waiting on her. He frowned when he thought about where she was. He wasn't thrilled about her not telling anyone where she was all the time. He wasn't even sure that Austin knew and he was her alpha.

Alexis came in the door just as her office door opened. Sis walked in, took one look around, and started for Gordon. No one said anything as she took his hand and led him to the couch. When she pointed to it, he sat down and she crawled up into his lap. Phil wasn't sure who was more shocked by the move, Alexis or Gordon. Phil decided they didn't really need him anymore and slipped out of the room.

~~~

Gordon looked down at the little blonde bundle in his lap. She was sucking her thumb and her eyes were closed. He could see her lashes as they fanned across her cheeks. He leaned down and buried his nose in her hair. Sunshine and warmth was all he could think about. He looked up at Alexis when she sat down across from him.

"She's never done that before. Not since my sister…she doesn't trust others since Judith died." Gordon had a moment to wonder if the child was more like her aunt than either of them realized. "When she died they were so lost. Darcy most of all, but Sis seemed to bounce back. At least during the day. She still screams in her sleep."

"Were they there? The children, were they there when it happened?" He knew that the boys hadn't been there. They'd been away at camp, according to what he'd read in the report from Dallas.

"Darcy was home from school for a doctor's appointment. Sis isn't old enough to go to school yet, and Judith couldn't manage day care on what little she'd get from the state. I told her that I'd pay, but she was very prideful and wouldn't let me." Alexis stood to take the baby from him. He stood with her and she led him out of the room.

They put her into her little bed. Gordon could see that the two girls shared a room. He could even tell which sibling shared what part of the room. The side that held the bed that Sis now occupied was covered in dolls and books, pink stuffed animals, and a bright pink spread. The room looked like a child played there. The other part was in deep contrast to this one.

The spread was a dark purple. That, as far as he could see, was the only color on that side of the room. It wasn't as though the room was done in black, but it was devoid of color of any other kind. The walls were white, the dresser and the desk as well. There were no books on the shelf, the bed was neatly made, and nothing was out of place. He looked at Alexis when she cleared her throat.

"She didn't want it any other way." She looked at the bed. "Nothing I could do could make her chose a color. The spread was picked out by Sis or she'd have a white comforter too." She nodded toward the door. "Let me show you out. Sis will sleep better if we leave her be."

Gordon followed her out without a word. He wasn't leaving her, not that night or any other night if he could help it. She was his and he needed to claim her before Patrick Booth hurt her. And he would once the pack started to come down on him. He'd do whatever he could to hurt her more than she'd already been hurt by him.

When they were in the hall leading to the front of the house he pulled her to him gently. When she started to protest, he kissed her. He didn't kiss her hard or even with as much passion as he wanted, but simply brushed his mouth over hers.

His body screamed for him to take her. His wolf, nearly at the breaking point, seemed to claw at him from the inside out. Gordon was careful this time to keep it slow; he didn't want to frighten her and he didn't want her to knee him again. When he moved to take another taste of her mouth he felt her stiffen. He didn't let her go as much as moved her behind him.

"Paddy, what the fuck are you doing here?" she practically snarled at the man in front of him. "You're not supposed to be within five miles of me and the kids. Get out before I call the—"

Paddy roared at her when she came around Gordon to get to the other wolf. It was all Gordon could do not to shift and take the man. He had his scent now and he'd pay for upsetting Alexis.

"It's time you left. Now." Gordon let a little of his humanity go to let the other wolf see that he meant business. He knew that this was the man who'd hurt his mate and also the man who was terrorizing the children, and it was now his job to protect them as much as he could.

The whimpering startled him for just a second. Before he could stop her Alexis was out from behind him and making her way to the sound. The man, Paddy, didn't move a muscle, but stood smiling at him. He smiled like he knew something that Gordon didn't.

"You the wolf who sprayed himself all over my future mate? You'd better stay the hell away from what's mine, little cub. I'm going to take what should have been mine in the first place, and you are inconsequential to my plan. The other one was a waste of my time." Paddy nodded toward where Alexis went without looking at her. "The scrawny one didn't tell me about this beauty before I fucked her. Had I seen her first, you'd be minus a bed buddy. And now that you've marked her it's every man for himself when it comes to claiming her."

He moved quickly and had Alexis in his arms before Gordon knew his intent. When Paddy stilled her struggles with a hand around her throat, she looked at Gordon with tears in her eyes. His wolf roared. Gordon felt the change coming. His beast wanted to kill.

"Let my mate go and I'll let you live long enough to apologize to her before I tear your throat out." Gordon felt his body respond to his mate's terror. His wolf moved along his skin and tore at him. "This is between you and me now. Let Alexis go."

Paddy licked her throat to her cheek. "Hum, delicious. I can't wait to have this sweet thing beneath me, screaming out my name. Do you know what I did to her sister? Do you have any idea what it felt like to kill her? You'd do well to remember I've tasted human blood in terror, little boy, and I'll have no trouble killing her just so you can't have her. Leave her to me and *I'll* be the one who lets *you* live."

The sound of a door slamming made them all freeze. Paddy jerked once as if he'd been hit. Then he leapt toward the door as a shot rang out, and Gordon could see where blood stained his shoulder. With a snarl toward something in the doorway, Paddy Booth shifted and leapt through the front door that was open.

"Find the kids and stay with them." Gordon looked to the door where the wolf had gone. "I'm so sorry about this." And he shifted. The last thing he heard before going through the still open door was someone screaming.

KATHI S. BARTON

# CHAPTER 6

Alexis paced. And when she wasn't pacing she was trying to comfort Darcy. The girl wouldn't let her touch her. Alexis glared at the people sitting on her couch and continued to pace.

"He'll be fine. I swear. He knows what he's doing." Alexis stopped and stared at Connor, Gordon's twin in every way. "He's been scrapping with me since we were pups."

"Oh, he'd better be all right. Because when he gets back here, I'm going to murder him." She started to pace again. "What the hell was he thinking running after Paddy like that? Does he think he's invincible? No, he is not. Stupid, moronic idiot should be...he should be caged or tied up outside so he can...what the hell are you laughing at?"

She turned on Dallas so quickly that he backed up in the seat. "Nothing. Well, except you sound just like CJ. She hated that Austin thought he was going to live forever too."

"So it's a wolf thing, this inability to be smart. I see." She didn't, but doubted she would ever tell them that. "I don't understand how your race has made it this far if this is how you handle situations."

"I don't think this is the time to be—" Austin stopped talking and stood up. His body looked as tight as a strung bow. When both Dallas and CJ stood, Alexis knew that something had happened to Gordon.

"You know something. What is it?" The hair on her arms stood when the baying began. It was just beyond her house, but it sounded like it was in the room with her. The sound at the front of the house startled them all and Darcy began to whimper. Alexis went to her immediately while the others made their way to the door.

Darcy knew something, or felt it. She'd been sitting in this corner since Alexis had managed to get the small handgun away from her. Where she'd gotten it was anyone's guess, but she was going to find out. She'd shot her father and had probably saved all their lives.

Alexis tried to calm her, but there wasn't anything she could do. She had to leave her alone to prevent her from hurting either one of them. She was struggling against even the smallest of comforts, and Alexis was terrified that she was going to harm herself. When CJ came back into her living room Alexis stood and nearly fell over when Austin came in carrying a large wolf. All hell broke loose.

"Stop that," Dallas snapped at Darcy. The keening stopped immediately. Alexis might have been mad, but the boys, who'd been awakened by the noise of the gunshot, needed her attention. She started to go to them when Connor said he had them and led them from the room. The wolf was laid on the floor near the fireplace.

"That's not...that's not Paddy. Who...?" She suddenly knew. "It's Gordon, isn't it?"

Alexis's hands began to burn and she put them behind her. She knew that at least one person in the room knew what was happening to her and maybe others, but she tried her best to hide it. Darcy was in no shape to tell on her. She looked up at CJ when she made her way to Gordon and was stopped by Phil.

"Will you do it?" She looked at the vampire and shook her head. "You can, can't you? You can save his life. I can hear his heart beating, Alexis, and it's slowing. He's been hurt helping you."

"What do you mean she can help him?" Austin turned to her, as did Dallas when Austin continued to ask. "Tell me what the hell he's talking about. What can you do to help my brother?"

"I can't do it. Please, you have to understand that...please don't make me do this. I've had to start over so many times." She felt the tears stream down her face. "Please, Phil, you can't want me to do this again."

She wasn't sure how he'd found out she could heal. She really didn't care at this point. But helping this man, this wolf, was going to change things forever. Too many people, all of them, could get her into so much trouble knowing she could do this.

"You have to, love. And no one here will condemn you. I'm not sure what you are, but you're not wholly human, are you?" She shook her head at Phil's question. "I thought not. Help him, Alexis, and if something happens to you, if anyone in here betrays you, I swear to you I will set it right."

She knew he was not only telling her he would protect her, but also warning the others. She looked down at the man on the floor. He was dying. She could hear his heart as well as anyone of them in the room. She dropped to her knees next to him and started rubbing her hands on her thighs.

"You'll have to tell my aunts that I've…that I took ill. I want you all to be gone when I'm through here. And I don't ever want to see any of you again. You've no idea what…it doesn't matter. If Paddy finds out, if he even guesses that this is what I can do, then there will be no stopping him. You understand?" She looked up at the people standing there.

"You save his life and we'll do whatever it takes to protect you. Whatever." She nodded at Austin. She didn't really believe him…she'd been made promises before and look where it had…she nodded again.

"Someone will need to make sure that he rests when you take him home. He'll be weak and tired for a bit, but he'll live." She looked down at the wolf and put her hands near his bloodied fur. "You people had better be true to your word. I don't want to run again. The children need me too much."

The pain ripped through her as soon as she touched him. She could feel each of his bites, each tear in his skin, and each place that the fur had been ripped from his body. She knew the exact location of the teeth marks that Paddy had given him, the depth of each bite, and even when the other wolf had shaken his head to inflict more pain. Alexis knew that she'd cried out; there was no stopping it. She hurt. She hurt as badly as the wolf, and knew that it was going to get worse, much worse.

Closing her eyes, she let her curse roll over her. It rolled from her into him, sealing the open gashes and mending the smaller ones. She had learned to breathe slowly when she did this or else the power would wear her out too quickly and the person would still need her help. She moved along his body. Each and every wound was sealed before she moved on to another place. The process was slow and draining to her, but she knew that as soon as she finished he'd be fine.

Exhaustion weighed on her when she opened her eyes. She had no idea how long she'd been helping him, only that she didn't have the strength to do much more than nod slightly at the glass of orange juice someone held out to her. She tried to speak, but before she could form words, someone picked her up and then blackness engulfed her.

~~~

Austin looked down at the sleeping woman in his arms. She'd saved Gordon. He didn't know how yet, but he planned to find out. He glanced at his mate as she pulled the blankets down off the bed in the room that one of the aunts had led them to. He was startled when Phil laid Gordon, in human form now, down on the other side of Alexis on the big bed.

"She has to mate with him now. If not, then she'll run." Phil covered Gordon up as he continued. "Please don't ask me what she is. First of all, I don't have a definite answer, and secondly…secondly, I don't think I believe it myself."

"You knew she could heal him. How?" Austin asked him. "What did you feel that none of us did? There had to be something that tipped you off."

"Something, yes. Let's take this downstairs. She'll be out for several days, her aunt said. The more…damage, the longer it takes for her to come back from it. They can't believe she did this again. They said she only does it for those she loves." Phil moved out of the room and they had no choice but to follow.

CJ stopped him just beyond the door. "She saved his life because he's her mate, didn't she? Even now she doesn't realize that she had no choice but to love him. Oh Austin, what happens to them all now? Do you know what she is?"

Austin looked back at the couple on the bed. "No. No, I don't know, but Phil does, and if he is this nervous, it can't be good. No, I don't know what she is, but I plan to find out. She's a member of this pack now, and we'll all protect her." He pulled his mate to him. "She saved his life. He was dying and she saved his life."

"I know, love. Whatever she is, she's very powerful. And yes, we'll all protect her."

The living room was nearly empty when they entered. Austin felt at home there. Not as much as he did at his own home, but he could easily see his brother living there with Alexis. Connor was sitting on the floor next to were Darcy was still hiding, and when Austin started toward him a small shake of his brother's head had him going toward the couch instead. He had never seen anyone as terrified in his life as that little girl. He wondered what had happened to this family and how they were going to help them.

"Alexis is very private, so what I'm going to tell you is something I don't believe she's ever shared with anyone but family." Glad sat on the couch as Jessie served sandwiches around. She took one off the tray as she continued. "Alexis and Judith weren't true sisters. Not by blood at any rate. Judith was Daniel's child and Alexis was Caroline's. The two of them, Daniel and Caroline, met when the girls were just about three. They married a few months later...Caroline and Daniel, not the girls. Both girls, head over heels in love with having a family, settled right in."

Jessie sat and picked up the tale. "When Daniel was away on business he had his brother, Donald, keep an eye on the house for his family. Donald had a son named Patrick Booth from an affair he'd had with a married woman. Sordid affair, it was, and the boy, Paddy he goes by now, became surly and resentful when he realized how happy the girls were. Don't know why, but he hadn't ever met Alexis as an adult or things might have been a bit different. She was away at school when she turned fifteen. She is as smart as they come, our Alexis, and she'd been offered all kinds of scholarships to go to all them fancy schools. But Paddy had his sights set on marrying up Judith when she turned seventeen and there was no stopping him. We both thought he was off his rocker, but then no one would listen to us."

"Wait, how are you related to her then? Why wouldn't you keep an eye on them if the boy was so bad?" Austin flushed. "I'm sorry. I shouldn't have—"

"Oh, it's all right. I was Caroline's aunt and Gladys here was Daniel's. We sort of became family when the two of them married." Jessie laughed. "Our family tree doesn't quite go in a circle, but it's pretty close. I guess you can say we formed our own pack."

Austin nodded. He was never sure what to do when someone outside mentioned his race. He wasn't ashamed of what he was, but he was fearful of others. He didn't remember a time when they had to outright hide what they were from humans, but he knew what could happen.

"Jessie, dear, do get on with it. The poor man is being polite and not telling you to get to the flipping point." Gladys grinned at him. "She dithers at times. It's sometimes difficult to keep her on point."

Austin felt his lips twitch. He was having a hard time keeping a straight face. But as soon as Phil snickered he laughed as well. These two women may not be related, but they sure knew one another well enough. He had no doubt that they would eventually get to the point, but it would take a trip through the wood on the way to the mall on the other side of the state to get there.

"Oh yes. Well," Jessie began with a snort to Gladys. "Alexis is a foundling. Do they use that term anymore? Oh well, she was a motherless child…oh, I do like that better. Motherless. Well, at the time she was found she was, but Caroline certainly never made her—" With a short nudge from Gladys, she moved on. "She was a beautiful child. And so good. We never told anyone, of course, just took her in and kept her. I was living with my Caroline at the time. We knew from the start she was different, but never really cared. Then later, Caroline met Daniel and it didn't seem to matter anymore."

"How?" Phil asked from his position at the fireplace. "What made you think she was different? Did she do anything...was she able to do anything that set her apart?"

"Well of course she did. What do you think I just said?" Jessie turned to Gladys and frowned. "Is there something wrong with the way I'm telling this story, Glad dear? Or is he, you know?" Jessie twirled her finger at her head to indicate that she thought Phil was crazy. The vamp growled, but was ignored.

"No, he's not, but you certainly must be. What did Alexis tell us about him? She said to behave around him because he's a...." Gladys lowered her voice, but they could all hear. "He's a vampire, remember?"

"Good heavens," Phil snapped. Austin laughed because the expression on Phil's face was priceless. Before he could get control of himself, Gladys whipped out a string of what appeared to be garlic and held it in front of him.

"I may be old, but I can certainly whip your ass if you think of having your way with me while you suck my neck, young man." Gladys looked so fierce that Austin pulled a pillow from the side of the couch and shoved it in his mouth. She looked like she could take on just about anything and come out on top.

Phil took the garlic from the older woman and tossed it across the room. "Let me guess, you've read about me in some smut book and now you think you have all the answers on how to keep me at bay. Well, ladies, I'm too old to be screwed with and I enjoy a very good garlic spaghetti sauce every now and then as much as the next person. Now, would you please tell us what made Alexis different from any other baby?"

"She was outside when we found her. Out in a basket with nothing more than a little bitty sleeper on her." Phil looked ready to explode before Gladys hurried on. "It was in the middle of winter. It was minus fifteen degrees out and she was laying there all warm and snuggly in her little basket. She'd been there long enough that the snow had no prints in it and there weren't nary a thing around her."

"The note, dear, tell him about the note," Jessie chimed in quickly. "It said that she was going to be hunted for her abilities and that she needed to be cared for and the person who loved her would be richly rewarded."

"Hunted how? I mean, it's not really telling you much, is it?" CJ frowned when neither woman answered her. "Surely it said more than that. Hell, I'm hunted now. There's that stupid guy who wants me to buy the property next to his so we can keep the unmentionables out. He looks for me every time he sees my car. What a moron."

"He wants to keep your panties from being exposed? Whatever for?" Jessie looked over at Glad before she continued. "I swear, every day people get more and more strange. Anyway, we came here. It was a lovely trip, wasn't it?"

Glad rolled her eyes and then she nudged Jessie again. "You're losing them again. Focus. They want to know where we came from. Isn't that right?"

"Yes," Austin said. "Where did you find Alexis? I'm sure if there had been anything in the paper I would have remembered. And what did the police say when you told them?"

"Oh my, as I said, we didn't tell anyone. That would have...they would have taken her, you see. So Caroline and I simply raised her as our own. She was such a good baby and a wonderful child. Very smart too. Then when Judith got married and then divorced and moved here from the Yellowstone area, we came with her. She was trying to hide out from that bastard of an ex-husband of hers. He was a bully, but it wasn't until he...well, changed that we knew how much." Jessie looked around the room as she continued. "Then after he killed our Judith and the poor homeless children needed more than...we're not exactly young chicks anymore, so Alexis dropped everything and came to help. She gave up so much, the poor dear."

"What did she give up?" They all turned to the doorway where Gordon stood. Austin didn't expect to see him for a few days yet and was very happy to have him up and about. Gordon brushed off any attempts of helping him as he made his way to the couch. He did lean slightly more on his twin when he simply shouldered him, but he sat down. He asked again.

"Oh my, she had a wonderful job. She was a chemical engineer. She worked at the space shindig." Jessie frowned. "No, that's not quite right. Is it?"

Glad shook her head. "No you old fool. It's space shuttle. Why do you take those memory pills if they don't work? You should do crossword puzzles or that Sudoku thingy. Keeps my mind sharp. Then there's the sex. I enjoy that too."

"Poo on them. Besides, I keep forgetting to take them. Space shuttle, that's it. She worked at the space shuttle. And then she stayed. What sex? With who? Never mind. I'm betting it's Wilbur Norris, that delivery guy who works down at the post office. He's cute. Then she bought this house and had it fixed up. She'd been making her scents forever at her old home and she continued them here. Opening that nice little shop has given us a place to play and to make a little money for ourselves."

Austin shook his head. He was going to need a scorecard to keep up with this family or, at the very least, to take notes. He wasn't sure what was being said, but thought he'd get with his family after they got home and compare notes. He looked around the room as one of the aunts began talking again.

"I doubt she'd miss us if we didn't get under her feet in the lab." Gladys turned to Gordon. "You know that she's given you a part of herself. And now that you have it, what do you plan to do to protect our little girl? Because now that she's given away her secret there will be a bigger chance of dumb ass Paddy finding out."

"Paddy will be back, won't he?" Gladys nodded at Gordon's question. "And when he does he'll not be so easily chased off and he'll come more prepared. He'll need to be put down, Austin, and we both know it."

"Oh my, yes. He needs to be put out of all our misery. And when you do...." Jessie leaned forward and Austin found himself leaning forward with everyone else in the room. "You need to cut his balls off and feed them to him."

Austin sat back and looked around the room. He wasn't sure who was more shocked by her statement. They all looked stunned. When she stood up all the men did as well, and she grinned.

"Oh my, how lovely. I'm going to fix us a late night snack. Would you gentlemen please go out and round us up a deer? You do that, don't you?" Jessie smiled. "Or perhaps you could go to the local market and get some steaks. It may be much quicker for us. Those sandwiches sure didn't last all that long."

With that, she went into the kitchen. Austin looked over at the stunned expression on Gordon's face, thrilled beyond words to see him sitting there. Austin grinned when he looked at him.

"Think of all the fun you're going to have when you and Alexis mate and become a couple. The fun will never stop."

Gordon groaned and Austin started laughing. Life for this couple may out do the one that he and CJ had. Especially when they figured out what the girl sleeping upstairs was.

# CHAPTER 7

Gordon watched her sleep. It had been two days since she'd healed him and she'd only moved in the big bed when he'd lay down with her. At first, she would move away from him, then about halfway through the first night she would lay close. Early this morning she was spread across him like she belonged there.

He looked down at the tiny pink scar on his leg. It should have still been an open wound. He could heal quickly, much quicker than a human could, but a break in his leg and the tears he knew had been there would have taken days to heal, not minutes. Looking back at Alexis, he wondered at what Phil had told him.

"She's told me she's not wholly human. I think that in order to figure her out…and please don't get pissy until you hear me out…I'm going to need to taste her blood. I won't need a great deal. A small drop will do me."

"What will that mean for you and her then? Will you be privy to our conversations?" As a mated pair of wolves they would be able to speak through their minds through a telepathic link. But a vamp could do that as well. He didn't want anyone to know their thoughts. Not ever.

"She and I would have a link, but the one between the two of you would be just that, between you and her. She isn't going to have to know if you don't want her to. I can never let her know that I'm there, just in the back of her mind." Phil began pacing, then he turned back to him. "You should tell her, or I can, but we can keep it from her if you'd like."

"No. If we decide to do this then she'll know. I don't want her to ever mistrust me and that stinks of lying. No." He watched as his brothers came into the room. They had information and it didn't look like good news.

"Patrick Booth paid someone to convert him about two years ago," Dallas said as he handed him a file. "He's also a vampire, which explains a great deal."

Phil spoke up then. "That does explain some, but there's more. He's been converted by a rogue vampire, someone that has been changing without permission. I thought... well, I had thought that Booth was something more than wolf when I smelled him on Alexis the first time I met her. You should know, Gordon, that he has beaten the children on occasion, and once he hit Gladys. I've seen firsthand what he's done to the little boy Tim. Alexis nearly killed him then. I have a suspicion that he may have a clue as to what his sister-in-law can do."

Gordon looked at her again as he took off his shirt. He wasn't sure when she'd wake, but he needed to touch her. Needed to be with her. Crawling into bed with her, he smiled when she moved closer to him then wrapped her arm around his waist. He had a feeling that when she woke she wasn't going to be so easy to be with. She was going to be one pissed off woman.

He lay there for some time thinking. He'd read the note that had been with her when she'd been found. It wasn't very helpful in figuring her out, but he could smell the person who'd written it. The writer's scent was as much a part of the paper as the woman lying in his arms was to him. And they were related.

Gordon wondered, not for the first time, what she was. Phil had hinted that she was something special. He already knew that. Gordon thought maybe the vamp already knew but was almost afraid to tell anyone for fear of being wrong. What on earth could make him think that he wasn't sure, but he could almost smell the fear. When she stirred he tightened his arm around her, fearful that she was pulling away.

He closed his eyes and smiled. Gladys had told him that tomorrow she would more than likely wake enough to go to the bathroom, and then it would be a couple more before she took food. Alexis had given so much of herself to him that he couldn't help but want her to wake now. But he also knew that her awake would mean an end to his sleeping arrangements. He slid into a deep sleep thinking about the child Darcy and her fear of her father.

His last thought before he drifted off to sleep was that Patrick Booth had a great deal of explaining to do and even more to be sorry about. And Gordon was planning to make the younger wolf feel sorry for a very long time.

"Come in," Gordon said to the office door when someone knocked the next morning. He was distracted or he might have looked up sooner when no one said anything. When he finally realized he wasn't alone he looked at Tim and Jake.

"We come to talk to you. You hit me or my brother and I'll whoop your ass."

Gordon fought the smile and leaned back in his chair, motioning to the two boys to take a seat across from him. He decided to ignore the cussing. This was going to be a serious conversation between men and he thought that it deserved serious words. "For the record, I don't hit. I punish, but not hit. You think I might have a reason to hit you?" The boys looked at each other, and it was then that Gordon realized that he'd never heard the other boy speak. "You have something to add to this, Jake, or are you the strong silent type?"

"Our mom is dead." Jake glanced at his brother before he continued. "We don't have nobody to keep us 'cause the mean bastard won't let them."

Okay, he thought, he was suddenly in over his head. Gordon looked at each boy and knew without a doubt that this was going to be the changing of their lives. They would either trust him after this or not, and he wanted their trust. He had a feeling he was going to be a huge part of their lives from now on.

"Why do you think your Aunt Alexis won't want you? By 'the bastard,' I'm assuming you mean your father?" Both nodded, looking relieved, he was sure, about not being in trouble about the name-calling or, for that matter, the word itself. "I'm very sorry about your mom. I love mine very much and I can see where you'd be worried. But I'm pretty sure you have a home with your aunt. She's trying to make sure that your father is out of the picture."

"He's very mean. Very." Tim said the word like it was a curse word. "And he…he can do stuff. Like we seen on television once. He can grow hair."

Gordon thought this was the perfect time to win their trust, or scare the shit out of them. He pulled back his sleeve and told them to come closer to him. He took a deep breath and let it out slowly.

"Okay, I'm going to show you something. Something that I don't share with many people, but I trust you guys to keep my secret. I don't want you to freak out." They both gave him the look that said, "Please, we don't freak out," and he smiled. "I can grow hair too. I'm a wolf."

He let the change move along his arm. The hair sprouted quickly, thick and dark. Both boys took a step back, but surprisingly neither of them ran from the room. Jake was the first to take the step forward again, but Tim ran his fingers along the fur.

"Can you change all over like that?" Gordon nodded at Tim's question. "Does it hurt? I mean, you can probably take it, but it's gotta sting a little bit."

Gordon grinned. "Sometimes it hurts when I have to do it quickly. Like the other day when I wanted to protect your sister and Alexis. But I didn't let it bother me. I had to see to the womenfolk."

They nodded, understanding the role of a man better than he had at their age he was sure.

"Do you get to bite people? You could bite our dad and we wouldn't care one bit. He's not a nice person and I hate him."

Gordon wasn't sure how to answer Tim's request so he let it go. He covered his arm back up and called his beast to him. It really didn't hurt. At times when he was really stressed, his wolf would appear just to remind him he could help out, but he'd never lost control of him. He started to tell them that they needed to keep his secret once again, but he could suddenly smell Alexis. She was getting closer to him.

"Your aunt is awake. She's coming here now." They were all staring at the door when it opened, and with wide eyes Tim and Jake looked back at him. "Maybe you guys should go and ask Gladys if she has a snack for you. I think your aunt and I have to talk."

They didn't hesitate but flew out the door like the hounds of hell were after them. Gordon couldn't blame them. He thought maybe he was in for it by the expression on her face. He stood and moved toward her.

"Hello, love. Sleep well?" He was only a foot away when she went to move away from him, but he pulled her to him before she got far. "No. I need to taste you first." And he brushed his mouth over hers.

~~~

Alexis wanted to tell him no, but her body seemed to know it was going to be a losing battle. She had her arms around his neck and her length pressed to his before she could make a sound. His low growl made her heart pick up in speed and her nipples peak under her shirt. When his tongue slid along her lips, she opened and let him in.

She'd been kissed before, but not a great deal, really. Her work had always come first. Men seemed to think she was okay looking, but she was usually bored to death by the first hour or so talking to them. Mostly she went to functions with people she worked with. When Gordon cupped her ass and brought her softness to his hard cock, she moaned deep in her throat. No one had ever made her feel like this.

"Do you have any idea how hard I've been, sleeping with you every night and not being able to make love to you?" He licked her neck and her entire body went into overdrive. "Alexis, I can smell you. Your heat, your arousal is making me ache to make you mine."

She pulled back slightly and his growl made her pussy wet. She couldn't seem to stop touching him, but she needed to make things clear to him. But every thought she had in her head flew out the window when he dropped to his knees before her.

"Gordon, you shouldn't—" Her pants were suddenly down and off. She was hanging onto his shoulder as he lifted her leg to remove them completely. Her body was like a live wire now. Need didn't just wash over her, but stormed over her like a torrential rain.

"A taste, love. I need to taste you." He lifted her leg and put it over his shoulder. She looked down at him as he said her name. "You belong to me, Alexis. Now and forever, you're mine. Say it. Say the words. Say you belong to me."

"Please, you've no idea—" He touched her inner thigh with his mouth. The kiss was wet, hot, and full of promise. She wanted him, wanted him to take her.

"Say it, Alexis. Say it for me so I can drink your sweet nectar and feel you come in my mouth." This time when he touched her with his mouth, he ran his tongue up to the elastic of her panties. She could almost feel him there, taking her into his mouth.

"I'm yours. Now and forever." She grabbed a handful of his hair before he took her. "But know this, you are mine as well, understand me?"

"I wouldn't have it any other way." The panties, the only thing keeping him from her, were suddenly floating to the floor behind him. He'd ripped them from her. Before they touched the surface Alexis was being devoured by him.

His hands seemed to be everywhere, and as soon as his mouth covered her mound she started to shake. He suckled at her clit and she cried out. Then when he slid his finger deep into her she felt the room tilt. Begging him now, begging him for everything and not really knowing what, she began to moan and ride him. He cupped her ass even as she started to undulate into his mouth.

Before she could protest when he pulled his mouth away, she found herself on the floor. He'd laid her down and had both her thighs over his shoulders now. Christ, she was in trouble. He ate at her like she was his last meal. Alexis palmed her breast. They ached, making her want to free them. Gordon seemed to understand, reached up with one hand, and ripped her shirt open for her.

"Let me see you. Open up and show me your bounty." His voice was husky and low. She found she didn't want to disobey him, didn't want to displease him. "That's it, baby. Christ, I want to suckle at your nipples, but your taste is all I can think about. Come for me, baby. Let me drink my fill."

She nodded. He grinned at her, sinful and full of heat. He moved his mouth down to her navel. His tongue swirled there, making her sensitive hollow a surprising erotic zone. She moaned when he nipped at her skin.

"Please, you have to do something. I'm hurting. Please," she begged him. When he sat up on his knees, her breath caught. "You're beautiful."

He ripped his shirt open and his chest was furred, muscled, and her mouth watered with want to touch him. When she started to sit up to do just that, he pressed her back down with a hand to her shoulder.

"Not this time. Next time you can have your way with me, but this time is for you. But I have to have a sample of you."

He crawled up her, not really touching her, but making her very aware of his heat. She could have reached up and touched him, ran her hands along his skin, but she waited, watched, and held her breath. He touched her with his tongue at her shoulder and she nearly came up off the floor. When he sank his teeth into her with just a bit of pain, she did grab his head and pulled him tighter to her. Her world was spiraling out of control and he was her lifeline.

"Please," she begged him again.

This time when he pulled away she sat up with him. Her hands made short work of his belt and snap. She wanted him now. He moved her hands and ripped the zipper out; zipper teeth pinged over the hardwood floor and were barely noticed. It was his cock, fully erect, that had her attention. He was thick and hard, and the stream at the tip of the engorged head made her lick her lips.

"I don't want to hurt you. I know you're a virgin, but I...baby, I don't know how gentle I can be entering you."

She was shaking her head at him even before he finished. "Alexis, this is a mating. When I take you, everyone, every supernatural, will know it."

"They'll hear us?" she asked him incredibly. Then she flushed, knowing immediately what he'd meant. But he didn't make fun of her. He only lifted her chin and took her mouth gently.

"Alexis, I know you don't want to hear this, but I'm in love with you. And I will never hurt you or any of your family." She tried to pull away from his words and his hand. "No, don't. I don't expect you to understand us. We're a breed of predators, but we love with all of our hearts. You have mine. Now and forever."

He took her mouth again and she was sure he could taste her tears. She hadn't realized that they were going backward until her back touched the cool floor again. He continued kissing her, his mouth moving along her jaw until he was at the place that ached for his teeth. She knew he was going to bite her, and she knew when he did it this time she'd be his.

He shifted again, and his hips rocked into her until she could feel the tip of his cock at her entrance. She wanted to beg him to take her. She canted her hips, hoping he'd get the message. He lifted his head and looked her in the eyes.

"Mine," was all he said as he plunged deep into her. Her scream tore from her throat. Not in pain, though there was a great deal of it, but from the climax that roared through her, over her. When he licked her throat she tensed, waiting for his teeth. He rocked into her again and again until she was nearing the pinnacle. When she dropped over the edge he sank his fangs deep into her as his cock spilled inside of her.

She heard him say, "mine" again just before she slipped into unconsciousness.

# CHAPTER 8

Gordon came awake in small degrees. First, he couldn't understand what was going on. The darkness of the room, the scents, were familiar to him, but not really home. He heard a moan, deep and full of heat, and reached for the woman who lay beside him. Before he could do more than move his arm he realized that he was hard and that she was over him. Reaching now for her hips, he came fully awake and sat up.

"Christ, you learn fast." He took her nipple in his mouth and suckled hard, letting it go with a small pop. He slowed down her ride over his cock and showed her how to do it. "That's it, honey. Slow and easy, slow and easy."

"You were so hard and you said I could—oh Christ, yes," she screamed when he rolled her to her back. "Pleaseohpleaseohplease."

Lacing his fingers into hers, he lifted her arms above her head. When he wrapped her fingers around the headboard, he ran his hands back down to her breasts. He moved in and out of her slowly even as she tried to get him to go deeper.

"Do you have any idea what waking up with you on my cock does to me? If you could manage to wake me up like this every morning for the rest of my days I will die a happy wolf." She whimpered when he pinched her nipple. "I love the noises you make when I touch you. The small sounds that escape when you don't want them to."

"You are going much too slow. I need to come. Please, Gordon, please help me to come." She grinned up at him. "I'll take your cock in my mouth."

"You will anyway, love. I saw the way you looked at me. Hungry. Are you hungry for me, Alexis? Do you want to feel my cum slide down the back of your throat?" He rocked a little faster, his game with her backfiring slightly. When she brought her hands down to him he stopped moving. She put them back and he rocked again. "My rules, love. I want to enjoy you tonight. You rushed me too much last night and I didn't get my fill of you."

"You bit me again." He felt her embarrassment, the heat of it. "Why? Why did you bite me again after you had already marked me?"

"Did I hurt you?" She shook her head no. He knew that he had, at least a little. "I had to mark you again because of that other wolf touching you. He…." Gordon took a deep breath, reining in his temper. "He licked you and marked you. A wolf does not do that to someone else's mate."

She turned away from him as he rocked deeper. He knew she was thinking and he didn't want her thinking of anything or anyone but him in their bed. He leaned down, took her nipple, and rolled it on the top of his mouth. When she arched up but held the headboard he lazily suckled at her while he pinched at her other peak. He lifted his head and waited for her to look at him.

"You need to know something. Something about me." He moved in and out several times, hard then slow, fast then softly. "Something important."

He smiled when she looked ready to brain him. "Tell me," she said between clenched teeth. "Tell me or fuck me, but for the love of Peter, do something."

"I'm possessive." He took her hard. His cock slid into her wet heat faster. When his balls tightened close to his body, the tingling in his spine telling him he was close, he leaned down and nipped at her ear lobe. "Bite me, Alexis. Please sink those beautiful teeth into me and bite."

The pain was surprising. He felt her mouth seal to his throat and she sucked hard. He didn't have a moment to think about what was happening. His body clenched tight. Then his climax grabbed him and soared through him quickly. He fucked her hard now, not stopping until she came twice then a third time before he collapsed on top of her. He barely had the strength to raise his head.

Blood was on her chin, his blood. His cock surged again, making him groan. When their eyes met she started to turn away and he stopped her with a word. She looked back at him with tears. He kissed her gently and laid his head on her breast, but not before glimpsing her teeth. His mate had canines like his.

~~~

Phil looked down at the notes he'd taken on the Dark family. There wasn't a great deal about them other than the few things he'd been able to track down at the county office in Montana. Then he picked up the second stack of notes. The Strong family, which he'd just happened upon, had a long and illustrious line. And he'd found out from his mother they didn't just have the last name as Strong, they were a breed of beings that were actual Strongs.

Alexis Strong Dark was a shifter…he just knew it.

He got up and walked around his desk. He loved his home and it had been his for over three hundred years. But he was lonely. Lonely for a mate and even lonelier because he knew who she was. Grabbing up his brief case, he went to the door and thought he'd try and get some more information from Austin on where Holly was. It was high time that little Miss Holly Force came to terms with who her mate was. And damn the girl for making him the heavy. Before he knew it Phil was knocking on the front door of the Dark home. Just as he thought, everyone was in the kitchen when he'd been let into the family home.

"You here for some home cooking, blood-boy?" Gladys had taken to calling him that a few days ago. He tried to not let it bother him, but today he just couldn't help himself.

"Yes. What type are you anyway? I've a craving for…." He sniffed the air. "Hmm, my favorite. Type B positive."

She paled slightly and he felt bad, but before he could apologize she slapped him on the shoulder with a hearty laugh. "You can't tell what my type is from sniffing the air. You're a card all right, Mr. Campbell. I think I might grow to like you."

He sighed. He was afraid she might grow on him too, and he just didn't want to think about losing another friend. He leaned in and kissed her cheek, giving a little of his magic to her. She would never know and he would have her around for a bit longer. He also made a mental note to do the same to Jessie.

He had the gift of longevity. Not many vampires possessed his power, especially not half-breeds such as him. He had given the gift to CJ and Austin, also to the other boys in the house. Nancy Force he had not. She knew that he'd been doing it slowly over the months and told him if he did that to her she'd hurt him.

"I want to go to my husband soon. Well, not soon, but when my time is right. You keep your voodoo and leave me to my own death." He'd kissed her cheek, but kept this gift to himself. "Now go and make me a grandma before I die, will you?"

That had been three months ago, and he was no closer to keeping his promise to her than he'd been back then. He walked into the dining room just as they were sitting down. He glanced at Darcy and knew that the girl was watching him. She was another puzzle he wanted to solve.

"Well, Alexis my dear, have you and your mate given any thought to my offer?" He needed her blood now more than ever. He was worried when she glanced at Gordon. He could feel the tension between them. "What is it?"

Gordon cleared his throat and handed a plate to Tim. "Why don't we bench this until after dinner? Then we can go out onto the deck and talk. And Tim here has an announcement to make."

The boy grinned, the first happy grin Phil had seen from any of the children since he'd met them. But something had happened to the couple at the head of the table. They would barely look at one another and they didn't speak to each other. He knew that they had mated, become a true mated pair, but their scent was different. It was more. Phil couldn't help but wonder if they'd found out something about Patrick Booth. But he doubted it would be that easy.

"I got an A plus on my math test today. Gordon helped me with figuring out how to add them up without using my fingers so the teacher would catch me."

"Really?" Alexis asked. "You taught him to cheat without being caught. Great. What's next, are you going to show him how to shoot your gun?"

"Can you?" Tim asked excitedly. He realized they were kidding about the same time Alexis shot him a look. "Oh. Well, that's not fair to get a kid's hopes all up then take 'em away."

"If you bring home two more As I'll show you how to throw a knife," Jessie said without missing a beat. "In my day I was quite the shot." She put peas on Phil's plate as she continued talking to Tim. "I could knock the eyeball out of a rat a yard away."

"Oh for heaven's sake, you could not. Why, you can barely thread a needle much less throw a knife." Gladys turned to Tim as she took the peas off Phil's plate. It was dizzying how fast the two women teamed up on his food. "You stay away from her, son, when she has a knife. She's more likely to cut your pecker off than to throw it with any kind of accuracy."

Phil looked around the table at the stunned faces. While the silence reigned he had a pork chop put on his plate and taken off, as well as a pile of mashed potatoes that would have fed a small army. He finally took his plate and moved far away from the two older women. He wasn't even hungry, but they were making him nuts with the switches.

Tim nodded and didn't say another thing about learning to throw a knife or shoot a gun. Phil did notice that he cupped himself whenever his aunt got close to him. The rest of the dinner was made in relative chaos, but the kind that he had seen in hundreds of families over the centuries. After dinner the kids were set up with a movie, and he went out into the warm night with the adults. Austin and CJ came just in time for dessert.

"How true is it that Caroline found Alexis and is not her real mother? Or you for that matter?" Phil would know if she was lying and could see the slight tension in Jessie's shoulders before she smiled at him. "If you lie to me, I will without a doubt know it. And will do whatever necessary to get the real truth from you."

The sharp intake of breath to his left told him that Gladys hadn't known, or at least he assumed she didn't. He was beginning to realize that this family had secrets that even he wasn't aware of. His quick glance at Alexis made him think she didn't either, but she'd suspected. Jessie looked around the group of people and then sat down hard in the chair next to her.

"She was Caroline's daughter. And before you ask me, yes, I know who your father is. We never meant for you to find out. It was supposed to be—"

"Wait. No, no, no. That can't be right. You told us that she was...you found her. The whole story was too wonderful to be...tell them you've made a mistake, Mr.

Campbell. Tell them that....” Gladys looked around and then at Alexis. “You knew, didn’t you? They told you.”

“No. I never knew. But there were times.... I look like her. I remember saying that to her once, to Mom, that I looked a great deal like her, and wasn’t that wonderful? She smiled at me and told me that it could be my curse too. That I would be recognized for that and that it could be her downfall.” Alexis looked at Phil. “Tell us what you know, and I’m sure that Jessie can fill in the blanks of what you don’t have.”

“I can’t. I know that you want the information, but I was sworn to secrecy. I have to continue to protect you until such a time that you’re called upon.” Jessie stood then sat again. “He’ll find you. Or at the very least he’ll come here. I’ve been watching over you for so long that...Phil, you should have asked me first and not told her. Why did you do that?”

The energy rolled off Jessie and hit Phil hard. It wasn’t the power that he was surprised by, but the amount of it. Jessie was at least part shifter too, and he knew that he was going to hurt very soon. He closed his eyes against the assault. But as the power slid over him it moved away just as quickly. He opened his eyes slowly. Alexis was standing before him.

“Stop it. Stop it right now.” Jessie stood, faced her niece, and then turned and walked away. The closing of the door was a soft click in the otherwise silent night. Alexis turned to him, anger in her eyes. “Tell me what you know. Tell me what I am and how you figured it out.”

Her voice was hard, but he could feel her fear. She really had no idea that what he knew was going to irrevocably change all their lives forever. He nodded to Gordon as he took a seat. "You've mated with her. You want to tell me what the problem is?" Gordon stiffened, as did Alexis. He knew that he was going to tell him it was none of his business, but right now he didn't care. "Jessie is right. Alexis is going to need help. If you aren't going to stand behind her or beside her, now would be the time to bail on her."

"She's my mate. I can't let her get hurt. Tell me what I need to know to make sure she's safe." Gordon glanced at Alexis then quickly away before he continued. "Our issues have nothing to do with whatever is going on right now."

"I bit him. He and I had sex and I bit him. With my teeth, and I...I drank his blood." Alexis looked at him as tears fell. "Am I part vampire too? Is that why he is so repulsed by me?"

"I never said I was repulsed. I merely said that you can't go around biting anyone else. I won't have you drinking from everyone because you didn't share you wer—"

"Shut the fuck up, Gordon." Austin stood up and shoved his brother in the chair when Gordon stood. "Sit down and shut the fuck up before I do it for you. Of all the stupid, asinine...what the fuck do you mean she can't...? Have you been paying attention to what's going on around us? You'd rather she die than drink from...? You fool. You don't deserve a mate."

"She's not a vampire. Not even a half-breed like me. And for the record, when Holly and I come together as mates, you so much as breathe a bad word to her about me drinking from her and I will tear you apart." Phil pulled out a file and handed it to Alexis. "Here you go, sweetheart. If you have any questions give me a call. I'm leaving. I wouldn't want to sully the air around here anymore."

He was around the house and almost to his car when he heard the first of the loud voices. Phil was too angry and too hurt to care what they did to each other anymore. He was going to find himself a woman and fuck her until she couldn't walk, then he was going to drain her simply because he could. When he was nearly home he had to pull over and take a few deep breaths. He couldn't do either of those things and he knew it. But he was going to wash his hands of Holly. There would be no way for him to be around the young wolf without remembering what her brother thought of him.

# CHAPTER 9

After she threw everyone out, including Gordon, Alexis went to her room and locked the door. She didn't do that often, but she really needed to think and she couldn't do that with everyone coming to her.

She started to open the file when she realized she was afraid. And she wasn't sure what was in the information, but whatever it was couldn't be good. Alexis glared at the file when her phone rang. After she picked it up she debated on whether or not to throw it at the wall, then gave in and answered.

"Can I come over? Actually, I'm here. Can I come down and talk to you?" Gordon sounded as resigned as she felt. "We have to talk, and I want to grovel to you in person."

She leaned against the coolness of her window, looked out into the dark, starless night, and watched the water fall over the stones a few feet away. She didn't want to deal with him tonight, if ever again, but if she hung up she'd have to deal with the file, and thought he might be the lesser of two evils.

"Why? If you really want to know the truth, I don't care what you have to say to me. I'm thinking you might be smart by staying away from me." She saw a movement out of the corner of her eye and watched as Gordon came into view, naked except for the cell phone at this ear. "What the hell do you think you're doing?"

"I left the pack house to go on a run and came here. I didn't have anything stored here so my clothes are still back at the place I took them off." He moved to where she was standing and put his hand near where her cheek was pressed against the glass. "I'm a fool. Worse, I'm a stupid, arrogant fool who should be shot."

"I'm not going to argue with you on any of that." She knew she couldn't really, but she thought she could feel his warmth. "I didn't know I could do that. I've never bit anyone before and you hurt me." She turned away from him to wipe at the sudden flow of tears. She looked back when he said her name through the phone.

"I'm more sorry than I've ever been about anything. You've no idea how much I enjoyed you biting me. And after...I said those things because I was scared. Not of you," he said hurriedly, "but of me. Christ, I wanted you to do it again and again, but I felt...well, I felt betrayed because you hadn't told me, then—"

"I didn't know. I had no idea that I could do that. The urge to bite you came over me so quickly and suddenly it seemed right. And, Gordon, you have...." She was almost ashamed to admit it so she looked down. "I came so hard and it felt so right to do it. Then you looked at me like I was a disease or something, and I couldn't tell you anything."

"Let me in, love. Let me in and let me make it up to you. I know what I did was horrible, and if Phil never speaks to me again or drains me it will be no less than I deserve. I'm going to spend the rest of my life trying to make it up to both of you, I swear."

Alexis looked at the only opening in her room that didn't come from the inside of the house. She hadn't told anyone about it and had had several contractors work on the emergency exit to ensure that the entire work was done so that no one but her knew the route. Did she trust Gordon with the knowledge, or should she just have him come into the house like a normal person? She looked back at him and nodded.

"Do you see the falls?" He nodded, turning to look at the small falls that hid the doorway. "Behind it is a split stone. When you step behind the water it will look like a solid wall, but the closer you get to it you'll be able to make it out. And once you get into the stone you'll want to make constant rights. I know that you'll think you're going the wrong way, but make all rights at every split."

He nodded then turned back to her with a grin. "If you're trying to get rid of me, will you please let my mother know that I loved her? She might not mourn now about my passing, but she may wonder a little later."

"She's mad at you, is she? Good. I hope she kicked your ass." He kissed the glass were she still was.

"They all did. So when you see my battered body in the light, know that I deserved every one of the bruises and I should have gotten more." He was gone before she could make a comment. His cell phone dropped where he'd been standing. She hoped that she hadn't made a terrible mistake when she saw him dive into the icy water.

~~~

The water wasn't just cold, but blue balls, my-blood-is-going-to-turn-to-ice cold. Gordon surfaced just below the small falls and climbed out where the water met the wall of stone. He was scaling the embankment when he saw the place he thought that she'd been talking about. He emerged behind the wall of water only to be faced with a sheer wall of rock.

Using his hands, he felt his way along the large stones. It was dark in the smallish cave, but he would bet that even in broad daylight it would be dark under there. He finally found the crevice and moved to stand in front of the opening.

It looked impossible for him to go through. His first thoughts were that she'd planned this to get rid of him. Then he took another two steps to stand to the direct right of the cliff and saw that the opening was incredibly wide. He stepped to it and slid inside.

He knew now what she'd meant when she said that he'd want to go left. First of all, the house was to the left. If he went left like he thought, he should be going toward the house, not away. Secondly, the way to the left was clearer and definitely brighter. Taking a deep breath, he started walking to the right.

The first turn opened into another small cave of sorts. There were lights coming from above and he thought he could make out a few bats hanging in the smallish alcove. He tried to ignore them, but there was just something very eerie about bats in a cave. He moved to the next opening and saw that if he went right again he'd be hitting a dead end. He started to turn around and go back, but remembered she'd told him to go right. He moved closer to the large wall and couldn't find anything.

Gordon was cold, wet, and tired. He'd had the shit beaten out of him by his brothers and his mom was pissed at him. CJ threatened to castrate him and Austin told him if he didn't fix this with both Alexis and Phil he'd have him thrown from the pack. And, he was beginning to realize that he could care less about any of that because, in the end, he'd hurt two people that were very important to him. He turned to go back out when he saw the opening.

It was to the right of where he'd come through. Not only was it well hidden, but the way it was situated made him think that he'd only seen it because he'd been about to slip against the wall. Had he not seen the small crease in the other stone he would have completely gone by it, and that would have made him lose his way. Clever, he thought. Smiling, he moved toward the opening and down a small set of stairs. When he got to the bottom, there stood Alexis. He stopped a few feet from her.

"I thought you'd changed your mind," she told him softly, and she bunched a towel in her arms. "I was just about to lock up when I heard you. Aren't you supposed to be very quiet when moving?"

"If I know I have to be." He took a few steps toward her, took the towel, and wrapped it around his waist. He knotted it at his hip as he continued. "Why did you have this built? Are you expecting trouble?"

"Always. I learned that I should always have another avenue of escape." She moved back when he was close and for now, he let her. "I'm still not very happy with you. Any of you, for that matter."

"You *should* be mad at me. I am an idiot and a fool." He ran his fingers down her cheek. "You saved my life and I let you down. Again. I'm sorry."

She looked away and he moved closer. When she moved back again he simply lifted her chin and kissed her gently on the mouth before moving into the room. And Christ, what a room it was.

He'd been there before, but he'd been seeing her for the first time in that white towel. Now he could see what Phil had said about the room was true. It was a work of art.

The windows that he'd been talking to her through were huge and showed so much of the outdoors. The only lights were from the moon reflecting off the water and the dewy grass. He heard her shut the doorway between where he'd been and the room, but was so focused on what beauty lay before him that he didn't turn. A half dozen deer walked into view as he watched.

"They come every night about this time. I think that the big boy, the buck, thinks I'm caged up or something and trusts I won't hurt his little family." She moved to his side as she spoke, but far enough away that he couldn't touch her. "Sometimes there are more, but always these few."

"They're hungry this time of year. It's too early in the spring for them to have enough food. But they look healthy and strong. They'll be foaling soon enough, and you'll have more than your little grove can handle, I think." He looked over at her as he finished. "You could move a few of the pairs over to my brother's land. They have several hundred acres there that they maintain."

She nodded and he turned to watch her look out the window. He looked around the room, wondering what other surprises she had down there. He smiled when he saw that she'd not only made the outdoors come into her room from the glass, but she'd brought a great deal of the forest in here too.

Her bed was made of fallen timber. He could see that someone had preserved the natural wood and had done so without losing the beauty of it. The four large logs looked to be from a variety of trees, and held a mattress that had been specially made to accommodate it. The walls were made of barn siding and looked to be an old oak. When she started to move away he reached for her and pulled her into his arms with her back to him.

"I'm sorry, Alexis. What I did, what I said to you, was horribly wrong and mean. I was afraid, terrified actually. Not of you, but…well, of me."

"I wouldn't have hurt you." He heard the past tense of the sentence and felt his heart skip several beats. "You should probably go. I have to look over this file that Phil gave me. He and I have an appointment in the morning."

"I want to help you sort it out. I need to. I won't sleep with you." He grinned at the expression on her face. "Unless you want me to. I'm not saying I don't want to, because I very much do, but you have to trust me and I know you don't."

She looked over at a small table tucked in the corner and he could see the file there. There was also a large wall unit that was closed up, and he'd bet that it held a computer and anything else she'd need for an office.

"I don't want you here. You're messing with…." She walked toward the door that he hadn't noticed before. "No one has ever been down here before except for the builders. You're messing up my karma, or vibes, or something. I'd really like for you to—"

"My wolf wants to touch you, smell you," he told her quickly. He didn't want her to send him away. "He's beautiful. And he'd very much like to meet you and not rush out the door like he did before. He snarls at me every time I can scent you."

She looked at him, but didn't tell him to leave. Yet. "You say that like he's a different person or something. Isn't he just something inside of you that you let out sometimes?"

"Yes and no. He's there inside of me, but he is a different being. He's the part of me that is beast. As for letting him out, I do when he wants. Sometimes for him and sometimes for me. He wants to meet you. He would never harm you. You don't have to be afraid of him."

"I'm not afraid of either of you," she snapped. He hid his grin by looking out the window again. He heard her move to the center of the room, but didn't look at her yet. When she spoke again, he turned slowly. "I can change too. Myself, I mean. I can change into anything I want, but I'm partial to an eagle."

He moved back slowly, trying to gauge when he was near enough to something to sit down or at the very least, lean against it. Gordon felt something hit the back of his legs and reached behind him to grab on. He was grateful when he realized it was a chair and that he was in the correct position to sit in it.

"How long...?" He cleared his throat twice before continuing. "How long have you been able to do that?" Thousands of questions popped into his mind while that many more tried to come to the front of the line. How? When? Why? Were only a few that he could get a fix on. He realized that she was looking at him and he tried to regain control of himself.

"You're mad again. Whatever." She moved to her bed and sat down. "I first changed into the eagle by accident. I'd been watching one in the backyard for a few days and wondered what it would be like. The next thing I know, I'm soaring through the sky with him. The next time, I really thought it out and felt it roll over me. The change, I mean. After that...." She shrugged. "I did it whenever I wanted to get away."

He nodded. He could understand wanting to get away, but that still didn't— "How old were you the first time? I mean, you make it sound as if you've been doing it for some time."

"I was six. It was right after my parents married." She stood up and started pacing as she told him more. "I didn't know why I could do it. And I'd always known that I was...Mom never lied to me about being adopted...well, she lied, but I hadn't realized she was lying. Anyway, so I didn't go to her about it. First of all, I was really afraid that she'd not want me anymore, and then later I didn't because it was something I had of my own."

"Do it," he told her softly. "Change for me."

She stared at him for several seconds and he knew she was going to tell him no. She nodded once and went to the door this time. He started to follow, but she stopped him at the doorway.

"No. You have to stay here and watch me through the glass. I can't do it with you too close. You'll make me nervous." She looked at the window and then back at him. "The sun will be up soon and you'll be able to watch. I won't come back here until…you'll be gone when I return, or I won't. It's as simple as that."

He didn't answer or move until she turned and walked away. He wasn't leaving. He wasn't even going to stay inside and wait for her to change. As soon as she was out of sight he closed her door and rushed to the panel he'd come through. Tearing off the towel and letting it fall to the floor he shifted and leapt to the first left. In no time he was at the falls and diving into the water as his beast. Coming up on the side, he shook the water free and looked skyward. Just as the sun crested over the trees, she flew over his head and took his breath away.

# CHAPTER 10

"Okay, tell me again why you can't get into the compound. Because the last I'd heard from you, it was a done deal. Nothing was in your way. You had her in the bag." Paddy looked at the man cowering before him and felt his fear wash over him like a very good drug. "But now," he said with a heavy sigh, "now you're telling me that it's not so easy to get to her and that...and how did you put it? Oh yeah, 'she's slippery as an eel in a tub of soapy water.' What the fuck does that mean anyway?"

"She's got her some guy living there all the time. He's a big fucker too. And he has this family I don't think you should be fucking with. Some say that they're all a bunch of wolves." Logan someone...Logan Glass, Paddy thought his name was, started nodding and all he could think of was that he'd like to snap his fucking head off. "And that lawyer guy? He's been telling people around town that he's gonna sic some heavy stuff on whoever tried to touch his friend."

Paddy knew about the pack. Hell, he was trying his best to get one gathered up himself. But he was having some...difficulties. Mostly it was because the current pack leader was a pussy and the wolves he had in his pack were loyal to him. Fuck that shit. Paddy wanted them terrified of him. Loyalty only got you so far before someone threw you under the bus and took your spot on the ladder up. Then there was the lawyer.

He'd heard he was a vamp. Paddy hadn't really believed in that sort of thing before and he hadn't dreamed there were werewolves, and now look at him. He stood up and stretched and took a deep breath of the fear rolling off the man in front of him.

Paddy started to pace. He knew that he had to get to Alexis before the fucking wolf she was mated to really claimed her. He needed her and the fucking kids that his first wife had given birth to.

Judith hadn't been the one he'd wanted, at least not after he'd seen Alexis. Where Judith was small and willowy, Alexis was an Amazon with her long, slim body and all that rich, dark hair. He wanted to fuck her every time he saw her. Reaching down, he adjusted his throbbing cock and smiled when Logan whimpered.

"Rest assured, you idiot, if I wanted to fuck you right now you'd bend over and drop your pants so quickly that my dick would still be tucked in my pants before you were begging me to fuck your tight ass." Paddy grinned as he stroked his cock and continued talking to the man. "She is to be here by Friday night or you'll pay the consequences. Do you understand me?"

"Yes. But how I gonna do that if'n she is locked down in that fucking house with—?"

Paddy kicked him in the face. He watched as the man rolled head over ass several times before he gathered himself up and cowered against the wall. Paddy needed to show this motherfucker who was boss and unsnapped his pants as he strode across the room. Before he got to the injured man he had his cock out and was fisting himself hard.

"Suck me," he ordered. Logan tried to make himself as small as possible by rolling into a ball, but Paddy jerked him up by his hair and pulled him to his cock. "Suck me off and I'll think about letting you live."

Logan only looked up at him and Paddy rubbed his cock over his mouth. He was so close to coming watching the blood drip from the man's nose that he almost simply came on his face, but the moment Logan's tongue licked at the tip of his cock, Paddy knew he wanted more.

He watched as Logan's tongue curled around his thick head. Still holding his hair, Paddy forced his mouth over his cock and moaned when he slipped inside. He rolled his hips, fucking Logan's mouth until he thought he might explode. His balls tightened to his body and he felt the first tingling of his climax racing up his cock. When Logan cupped his balls and rolled them in his hand, Paddy came. And came hard.

Dizzy with his sexual release and that fact that he'd come in a man's mouth, Paddy put his hand on the wall in front of him and leaned against it. He closed his eyes and tried to shut out what he'd done. Anger surged through him and he lost his temper, something he'd been doing more and more lately. Jerking Logan up with one hand, Paddy jerked his head back and bit deep into his jugular.

Hot, fear-spiced blood poured down his throat. He barely noticed when Logan began to struggle less, noticed even less when he lay limp in his arms. When Paddy had his fill he simply dropped the man on the floor and stepped over him toward the door. He needed a woman right now and he had not a care in the world who it was.

The first female he saw was his cook. Not saying a single word to her, he slammed her against the counter where she was cutting something up. He took the knife from her hand, threw it toward the wall, and barely noticed when it stuck there and quivered from the strength of the impact. Taking her pants in his hands, he ripped them off her and bent her over. Before he could enter her, he heard a scream and knew it wasn't from her. Turning, he saw a movement and a quick streak of color, and then something hit him hard. Paddy had a moment to realize that he should take more care when he did things with a witness. His eyes closed as he slipped away, the feeling of blood pouring from his head.

Paddy woke slowly. The silence around him was profound. He knew that he couldn't have been out long or he'd been out long enough for it to be night again. He could see the moon streaking across his body from where he was laying. Moving gingerly so as not to make noise, he stood up.

His pants were still down around his thighs and his shirt was bloodied where his head had bled on it. He reached up and found that other than a tender stop on his temple, he was fine. Adjusting his clothes, he moved through the house toward his office.

He didn't see anyone, nor could he smell anyone in the house. Death was there, and when he found Logan slumped on the floor where he'd dropped him, he wasn't surprised. Glancing at the clock in the corner, he realized that maybe an hour had gone by. He looked at the body again and wondered if the others of the house, two others besides his cook, had seen Logan there and if he'd have to be explaining what had happened to the police. Probably not, but he still picked up the body and took it to the rear entrance of the room and out into the darkening yard. Heaving the body into the bushes, he looked up at the waxing crescent.

The new moon was nearly here. He needed to get to Alexis before then. If not, he'd have to give her up. And as much as Paddy wanted Alexis for his own, his master wasn't going to be denied. That was Paddy's price for being changed into the marvel that he was.

Tom Garrison was an old and feared vampire, and a person who made things happen. When Paddy had first come to him about being turned, he'd turned him down. Then Tom had seen his daughter Darcy. And then his ex-wife Judith.

"I'll tell you what, you bring me your wife and I'll convert you. I won't even charge you my usual fee if you bring her to me before the next moon phase." Paddy was already thinking of ways to get her to him as Tom continued. "And if you throw in the daughter, I'll change you to a wolf too."

He hadn't even asked why he needed his daughter too, but said he could get her as well. Paddy was changed the next week, and had gone to his wife's home to get them when all hell had broken loose.

~~~

105

Alexis knew it was Gordon the moment she landed in the branch above him. He looked so big sitting there as a wolf looking up at her, and she thought maybe he'd just move on, but the longer she sat waiting for him to leave, the more relaxed he seemed to get until he simply lay down on the ground and watched her.

She might have screamed her frustrations out but she knew that she couldn't, and stomping her foot wouldn't work either. A bird couldn't do either of those things. Alexis dropped down to the next branch, then the next, until she was nearly on top of him. The thought of swooping down over him, maybe taking a chunk out of his fur came to her, but she was sort of afraid that he'd snatch her out of the air with his teeth. Knowing that he said he wouldn't hurt her was one thing; whether or not he would do it was a different matter altogether. Then there was the fact that she would be naked if she shifted back.

Still in the tree, she wondered again why he had come out here. She'd hoped that if she told him she could change into a bird he'd be repulsed and leave. She should have known he wouldn't be that easy to get rid of. Sighing heavily, she moved down another branch. When he yawned and closed his eyes, she screeched. Alexis wasn't sure, but she thought he was laughing at her.

This time when she moved, it was to the forest floor. She sat watching him as he opened one eye then the other to look at her. Still he didn't move, didn't even so much as stretch out. The noises of the area around them seemed to still and she looked to her left when she heard a small noise. Looking back at him, she was surprised to see that he had shifted back to human.

"You're a very beautiful eagle. But then, you're a very beautiful woman, so it really shouldn't have surprised me." He laid on his belly, his head resting in his hands as he leaned on them. "Can you understand me?"

She nodded before she could think to pretend that she couldn't. His grin made her think he knew that he'd caught her off guard, and she thought she'd have to be more careful in the future. He was tricky.

"Trust is a very fragile thing. And I know that I've hurt that between us. You've no idea how sorry I am for that. You've been nothing but honest with me from the very beginning, and the one time you let yourself go with me, I do the most incredibly stupid thing and hurt you." He picked up a blade of grass and she watched as he twirled it in his fingers, remembering when he'd touched her with them. "When Austin met CJ he ordered her around and told her what she was going to do and that she was going to listen to him no matter what she wanted. Of course, you've met her and you know how well that went over. I swore to myself that I'd be a more understanding mate, someone that my own mate would love without thinking I was an overbearing asshole."

Alexis thought about what CJ had told her and what this man was saying. CJ had said that Austin had some major lessons to learn when they'd first gotten together and that he'd had a list of things that he felt she should follow. She'd told Alexis that she'd taken the list, read it over, then tossed it in the fireplace. Then she proceeded to give him the cold shoulder and the cold bed. CJ did admit that she thought that was harder on her than it had been on him, but said she'd never tell him that.

"If you shift, I promise that I won't jump you." He grinned as he sat up and nodded to his hard cock. "As you can see, I want you. I want to take you right now, here in the forest like you were made to be taken. But I want to talk to you. We need to talk."

She looked around. Shifting for her was easy, but still, being naked around this man made her think she would be the one jumping him and not the other way around. He groaned softly and she looked up at him as he stretched his massive arms over his head and then rubbed his furred chest as he settled back on his hands.

"I can smell your arousal, love. If you shift back, we can make love, then talk. The thought of burying my cock deep into your wetness makes me harder than I've ever been." His legs moved out to the front of him and he looked at her. "Come to me, Alexis. Come here and take me."

Without thought to what she was doing, she shifted and stood. She stood there for several seconds just letting him get his fill of her. When she took a couple of steps toward him she thought he'd move to grab her, but he only waited. She was standing before him before he spoke.

"Christ, you're beautiful. More beautiful than anything I've ever seen. Come here, love. I want to touch you." She wasn't sure what to do so she moved to stand between his outstretched legs. When he reached up and pulled her to him, he buried his face against her thigh. "You smell like heaven to me."

She rubbed her hands through his hair and tightened her grip when he licked her. She felt her pussy walls clench and when he moaned, she moaned in return.

Moving to sit on him, she straddled his legs. But before she could sit, he pulled her around so that he was looking up at her from between her legs.

"Gordon, please. I want you to taste me, eat me, please? I need you to help me come." She widened her legs when he ran his hands up her inner thighs. "Please, I ache for you, need you."

His tongue lapped at her thigh again and she held him to her. When he slid his fingers up her leg and brushed against her nether lips, she closed her eyes; the feelings were so overwhelming.

"Open your eyes. Watch me lick you. Watch me, Alexis, while I drink deeply from you." She opened her eyes and looked down. "I want you to come in my mouth, then I want you to ride my cock until I fill you with my seed."

She knew that she'd not last. Once he touched her she knew that she'd come quickly. Watching him, she tried to think of anything else, anything but what he was about to do to her, do with her. When he cupped her ass and slowly brought his mouth to her, she cupped her breast, suddenly needing more.

His tongue moved over her relentlessly. Over and over he skimmed her clit, never touching her where she needed, not even coming close to letting her get relief. When she tried to guide him to her, he chuckled as he slid his finger deep into her sheath and her legs trembled with need. Begging him now, she rocked into his mouth.

"Gordon, I'm going to murder you. Give me what I— oh, Christ, yes." She came quickly when he suckled at her clit. Even as his tongue and fingers filled her, she felt her cream run down her legs, her body seemingly getting ready for him again.

Guiding her down over him and onto him, she took his mouth when she was across him. His fingers dug deep into her ass as he pulled her to him.

"Ride me. Slowly. I want to savor you." He grinned suddenly. "Savor you for as long as I can."

Wrapping her legs around his hips, she rolled her body against him. He filled her, his cock touching her deep. His mouth was everywhere, touching and tasting, nipping and biting her. She moved her mouth along his throat, nearly taking him again. As she started to pull back, he cupped the back of her head and held her to him.

"Bite me. Drink from me while I release my wolf enough to mark you. He needs to make you his." He ran his tongue along her neck where her shoulder met her neck. "He will mark you, scar you, and make you his. Take from me, Alexis. Take what I offer and make me yours."

Her canines elongated. She felt them burst from her gums and her mouth watered to drink. She heard him snarl and looked up at him. He had changed. His eyes had darkened, his canines were there, long and sharp. She felt her climax rising and when he snarled at her to take him, she sank her teeth into his throat and felt him do the same to her.

# CHAPTER 11

Darcy watched the couple come into the house. She didn't move from where she was, but knew the moment that the man saw her. She stepped out of the dark corner and looked at him. He was huge, but he didn't frighten her, not like her father did...at least not as badly. He didn't snarl and snap at her either, which she was surprised about. Her father always did.

"Darcy." He moved slowly and she was still afraid, but not terribly. "Are you okay? Your aunt and I are just going to get something to eat. Would you like to join us?"

She didn't answer him, but she did move to follow them. Her aunt put her arm around her and she stiffened, but Aunt Alexis didn't pull away. Darcy knew that she should do something...anything to let them know she was okay, to at least make them stop worrying, but she wasn't sure what *was* wrong with her.

Bits and pieces of what happened had come back to her. She was remembering more and more all the time, but what it all meant was still foggy. There was a large dog, but somehow she knew it was more. Then there was redness. She felt a pain in her head when she thought of the redness, and was nearly blinded by it when she thought of her mother.

"Have a seat, sweetie, and I'll get you something to drink too." She glanced up at Aunt Alexis and then back at the table. She felt shame for something and wasn't sure what it was.

"Darcy, look at me," the man said to her and she obeyed. Once she looked into his eyes it was like she couldn't look away. "You're going to be safe here. I won't let anything happen to you. I'll protect you all."

She found that she wanted to believe him. More than anything she wanted to, but there was something that she knew, something that she was sure was going to come and get her. She looked back down at the table when she felt the release and then put her hands on the table.

The pictures she'd been drawing. If she could make them look at them she knew that they'd understand what she wanted. Death. If she could just simply die then she'd be better. She glanced over at the knife, the one she'd been coming down to get when they'd come into the house, and wondered if she could snatch it up and plunge it into her chest before they could stop her.

"There's a festival this weekend at the high school. I thought we'd go and check it out," the man…she couldn't remember his name…said. "The weather is nice enough, but I think it'll rain."

Aunt Alexis laughed and Darcy looked up quickly to see if she was laughing at her. But it was the man…he was tickling her aunt. Darcy started to get up, to leave them, but the man put a plate in front of her and said to eat. Picking up the bread, she played with the crust.

*Tell them*, her mind screamed at her. *Tell them, tell them, tell them*. She wasn't sure what she was supposed to tell them, but she knew that sooner or later they were going to need it. Glancing at the man again, she stood and left the room. The pictures were in her hand and she was back in the kitchen before she realized what she was going to do.

"What do you have...?" He lifted her chin when she continued to look at the table after handing him the drawings. "Did you draw these, Darcy?"

She pulled away from him and picked up the bread again. She didn't know what the pictures were, she wasn't even sure if she'd drawn them, but she had them and when she looked at them, her head hurt. She knew when her aunt had looked at them. The sharp intake of breath was all she'd done, but the man, Gordon she suddenly remembered, sat next to her at the table.

"These are very good. I'm impressed with the detail in them. Is this a wolf?" She glanced over at the big dog she'd seen on the top most pictures and went back to her sandwich. "And this one, is this your house?"

She didn't answer him, but she heard her aunt tell him it was. The house she'd been in before, the one she and her sister and brothers had been in. She took another bite of the sandwich and listened to them.

"They lived there most of her life. It's the house her mother got in the divorce when they...when Paddy left them. They've only been living here since I had the renovations finished. Before that they all lived with Aunt Glad and Aunt Jessie." Finished now with the sandwich, she picked up the glass and stared into it as Gordon sorted through the pictures. He continued to talk to her.

"Darcy, can you please tell me about this one? It's a very violent picture, and if you tell me about it, I can try and help you make sense of it." She glanced over at the picture then back at the glass of milk. "I think you know more than you've let on. You know about your father, don't you?"

"Don't," her aunt said, but Darcy got up and looked over his shoulder at the picture. When her aunt started to speak again, Darcy put her hand on Gordon's shoulder and held on. Aunt Alexis moved to the other chair and didn't speak again.

"This one shows a man changing into a wolf, I think. I can see his paws here and I think this is his fur. Paddy is a brown wolf so I'm assuming this is of him." Darcy started to nod, but didn't. "And I can see his canines. Did you know that that's what wolves' teeth are called?"

Darcy knew that, but didn't answer, as much as she wanted to. She found that for the first time since she'd awakened in this house she wanted to say something. Darcy rubbed her hand over his shirt and felt his warmth. She moved closer, feeling...safe for the first time since she was little.

He was handing her a pencil and she took it. Before she knew it, she was sitting at the table again and had a sheet of paper in front of her. Her mind drifted away and her eyes became unfocused. Blurry images seemed to come into sharp pictures, and then she was crying. Then when she felt someone hugging her, she wrapped her arms around them and held on. It wasn't until later, when she was nearly asleep, that she realized it was Gordon that held her, and Gordon and her Aunt Alexis who put her to bed. She closed her eyes and fell into a deep sleep even before they left the room.

Darcy sat up, sweat drenching her and her eyes wide with fear. Breathing hard, she looked around the darkened room and searched. She wasn't sure what she was looking for, but knew, just knew that it was right there with her. When she saw the bright eyes she whimpered and pulled back on the bed. Suddenly he was on the bed licking his lips, and that's when she screamed. Screamed over and over until the lights came on and she was jerked up from her bed.

"It's all right. I've got you. Come on, baby, wake up. I've got you." Aunt Jessie was holding her. There were others in the room, but Jessie was holding her. "Open your eyes, come on, Darcy. You scared fifty years off me; good heavens, girl."

"It's the drawings. I was worried about that, and I told you no good could come from it," her Aunt Alexis said. Gordon came to the bed with her and sat there, smiling at her. "You should be whipped."

"She thinks she can whip me. I think I can take her. What do you think?" She looked at Gordon then back up at her aunt, who was pacing. Neither of them seemed really mad, but she didn't know. Darcy pulled the blanket up and started to lie back down, but Tim came into the room and hopped on the bed with her.

"If everybody is up, do you think I can have some pancakes and waffles? I'm really hungry." Tim held her hand and she looked away, but back at him when he started to fib about her. "Darcy and I been talking, and she really likes pancakes and waffles together, don't you?"

He winked at her. Then Darcy looked over at Gordon who winked as well. She nodded once then started to get up, but Sis tackled her first.

"She talked, didn't she? Darcy can talk again. Come on, Darcy," Sis said to her pleadingly. "Say my name and I'll give you my favoritest dolly. The one that Aunt Jessie made for me. Please? Say 'cat,' just like that, 'cat.'"

Darcy looked up at her Aunt Alexis and the connection was suddenly there. And then the memories flooded her mind. The dog was a wolf, but there was a man too. Big and mean, and he had a cane. Aunt Alexis came then and she was covered in red; not paint like she'd thought, but blood. Her own. Aunt Alexis had gone after her dad and he'd...he'd hurt her. The man with the cane had hit Darcy, hit her so many times that she hurt for so long, then nothing. Then she'd awakened in the barn at her mother's house.

"You saved me." Darcy was startled by her own voice, but she said it again, said it to the woman who had put her hands on her and saved her. "You saved my life, but couldn't my mom's because you said she was too far gone."

~~~

Paddy paced outside the gate. He wanted in and he would have been in except for the hum of electricity that told him that scaling the fence would get him hurt badly. He was waiting for someone, anyone to come out of the gate and he'd slip in. Of course, that had been the plan over three hours ago. Now he just wanted to hurt someone.

He was afraid, not that he'd admit that to anyone but himself, but the police showing up at his door shortly after he'd gotten back in the house made him realize that he shouldn't have killed Logan. And raping his cook, or almost doing so, didn't seem like such a good idea now either. But they had hurt him. She, or someone there with her, had hit him hard enough to make it so that the cops had almost gotten him. He hoped that they got what they deserved.

There were other wolves around the compound and he could smell even more that had been around recently. Even in his young life as a wolf he knew that one of them was powerful...an alpha if he didn't miss his guess, and one of great strength. He wondered, not for the first time, if it was the one who'd marked Alexis, but he'd missed cataloging the scent and now he was lost. He was still learning more and more every day, and making mistakes, especially one like that, made him angry.

The car coming down the road made him pause. He watched as it drove by slowly but didn't stop. Didn't these stupid people need to get stuff or something?

Food, for one thing. He had been here for several hours off and on and couldn't believe that not one person didn't need to get something from the store or just to get out into the open. He'd been to the store down the street three times since the crack of dawn, and still nothing from the people inside.

Another car came down the street and this one slowed in front of the gate, but drove on. The prick was teasing him and Paddy just knew it. If he wasn't so afraid of missing the chance to get inside, he'd have gone after the driver and torn him to bits just to prove who the bigger man was. Smirking, he wondered what the guy would do if a big, bad wolf jumped in front of him. Probably piss himself.

Paddy tried to shake the feelings he was having. Terror and anger, meanness and hatred seemed to roll over him in waves until he had no idea what to do other than just let them go. The worst was his need to fuck. Everything that walked, and it mattered little to him what the sex was either. He started to pace again and looked at his latest problem. The gate was keeping him from getting what he wanted.

The monstrosity behind him was made of stone and metal and, in addition, electricity. He was left wondering who the hell she'd been trying to keep out when Alexis had had it installed. He knew it was more than likely him, and then smiled when he remembered why she'd been trying to keep him out. He'd tried once before to get in, before the fencing had been put into place, and that hadn't gone well. All that had gotten him was a workman trying to shoot him. The ignorant ass had had a small peashooter on him at work, for Christ's sake.

He'd followed the worker home after that. He'd found him outside the gates and made sure the idiot never shot at him again. Of course, that had earned him a swift and horrific punishment from the guy paying the bills, but it had been worth all the pain to taste his first human blood.

He began thinking of one of the other times he'd tasted blood. It had been his ex-wife's, and it hadn't been as sweet as he'd hoped it would be. Terror made the blood rich and spicy. Judith's was hard, bitter, and a little on the sickening side. She'd been protecting her cubs, Tom had said, and that made her blood nasty. He would know, Paddy supposed. He'd been around for a long time. Frowning, he tried to remember more of what had happened at the house, but drew a blank.

Alexis must have been there when he and Tom Garrison had shown up to get Judith and Darcy. Judith had been packing a van with suitcases when the two of them had come to the house. When he'd been trying to scare his wife into cooperating with him, Alexis had come from nowhere and jumped him. Paddy hated Alexis after that. Didn't mean he didn't want her, but he did hate her.

Paddy knew that she'd hurt him that day. He wasn't sure what she'd done to him, but when she'd hit him it had hurt more than anything he'd ever had happen to him. He told Tom that she'd stabbed him, but he swore that she'd only touched him. What the hell did he know anyway? The pain had been stab-like, not touch-like at all.

He'd lost control then. His wolf had sort of jumped out and taken over his body and mind before he knew it was even possible for it to happen. Things had blacked out for a time after that. When he'd come back from his wolf he was in the back of a car and it was speeding down the road. His naked body was covered in blood and his head was pounding. Tom was staring at him with mean eyes when he looked up at him, and before he could ask what had happened, the cane the man always carried was coming down across his head. He was out again before he knew it.

The next time he woke he was in a cage and still a human. While there were people all around him, none of them made any sort of move to release him. There was a guy in a lab coat, a pretty nurse he instantly wanted to fuck, and Tom.

"You really fucked up this time, Patrick Booth. You fucked up so bad that I had to use my considerable resources to clean up your mess." Tom had come to the cage and rapped the cane on the metal and Paddy jumped back. "You need to learn your place, young man, and starting with that young woman who came in and had the nerve to knock me down."

Paddy didn't remember that, but then he didn't remember much when he was a wolf. He moved to the middle of the cage and looked up at Tom.

"Why am I in here? I didn't do anything you didn't tell me to." At least he didn't think he had. And if he had, he was pretty sure that he'd be dead now and not just in a cage. "Let me go and we'll talk."

Tom sat back down in his chair and waved the others out. The nurse looked at him and it was then that he could see the hatred on her face. He tried to think what he'd done to her too, but the door was shutting and he looked back at Tom.

"You killed that woman. Your ex-wife, she's dead. You went nuts and...well, I'll be lucky if I can ever get the stains out of my suit. You'll be paying for that, you can bet. Dry cleaning blood out is a no-no. So, I'll expect you to compensate me nicely. As for her death, it is my understanding that wolves, once they get a taste for blood, never can get enough."

Paddy sat back on the wall and took several deep breaths. He'd killed Judith. He didn't remember, but he was sure that Tom was telling him the truth. He looked up at the man.

"How? I mean, how did I kill her? And the kids, are they okay?" He wasn't sure what Tom had in store for his daughter, but he was pretty sure it wasn't good. "I think I'd like to change my mind about Darcy. You can't have her now."

The cane hit the cage again, this time so hard that it rattled him too. When he scooted back this time, he was afraid. He was suddenly very afraid not only for Darcy, but for him as well.

"You'll give me what I want or else I'll hurt you in ways you can't imagine. I will make your conversion seem like child's play compared to what I'll do to you." He sat back again. "You are going to get me the child. And you'll get me the woman that knocked me over and took the child from me. She will pay for her...indiscretions. The girl, she'll be my day walker and someday my bride."

Paddy remembered shuddering, thinking that he didn't want the vampire to touch him much less his daughter, but a deal was a deal and he didn't want to be hurt. Darcy would have to be on her own, he reasoned. She was smart, she'd learn her way. Paddy nodded and after a bit more conversation, mostly from Tom, he was let out. That had been just over two months ago.

After another hour of nothing moving in and out of the driveway, Paddy shifted and ran to his car. He hated that he had to go back to human form to get inside his dive of an apartment, but there was no hope for it. The first time he'd tried to get inside as his wolf, the neighbor, a nosey bitch, had called the police and he'd been chased out. Since then he'd made sure he made a great deal of noise when he heard them go to bed and when they'd complained, he'd met them at the their door as a wolf. They didn't complain any more.

His cell phone was ringing when he entered his shabby room. He hadn't taken it with him because he didn't want to give away his position hiding out. He looked at the caller ID and didn't recognize the number so he let it go to voicemail. Stripping down, he stepped in the shower and was drying off when he heard it ring again. This time he answered, ready to give the person on the other end a piece of his mind.

"They know. They found out that you killed your wife and they're going to come and get you." The call ended with a bang. He set the phone down then picked it up to dial to retrieve messages. It said basically the same thing, only this time there was a threat. "If you tell on me, I'll take you down with me."

Paddy sat on the toilet and set the phone gently on the sink. He stared at it for several seconds before he leaned forward, rested his head in his hands, and continued to stare. He didn't have any idea who it was and worse yet, he didn't know what the hell they were talking about. He moved out of the bathroom then started to get dressed. He didn't even go near the phone until he was completely clothed and had his boots on. He picked it up and decided to call the number.

It rang three times before someone answered. It was a woman this time instead of the man from the other two calls. He waited for her to say something besides hello, but she didn't. Then when she did speak, his entire body chilled.

"It will do you little good to figure out where this call came from. You'll still be dead. Dead sooner if you fuck with us." There was a shuffle of something heavy then, "Call this number again and I will hunt you down and cut your pecker off."

The line going dead was nearly as scary as the threat.

# CHAPTER 12

Glad watched the children. She'd been trying to think of a way to talk to her grandniece, but all she thought about was that Darcy was talking only to Gordon and Dallas about what had happened. And what she was saying to them was…well, Glad's heart hurt not really knowing everything.

Someone had come into the house and had killed Judith. They knew that. They'd thought it was Paddy, but it turned out that he'd actually been knocked out when it happened. Darcy had said that he'd changed into a wolf and that he'd attacked them, but the other man had shot him with some sort of gun and the needle had been sticking out of his fur when he'd gone down.

The man, Tom is what Darcy had said her father had called him, had then attacked Judith, who was trying to hide her. Darcy said her mother had been shielding her with her body, but the man had simply used the cane that had changed into a large sword. He'd cut her nearly in half, and after she'd fallen he'd started beating on Darcy.

"He cut me up really bad. I was bloody everywhere and then he stabbed me in the chest. I tried to get away, but...but I fell, and then Aunt Alexis came into the house. She tried to get him off me, but he wasn't having it." Darcy looked up at Glad and then away. Glad was afraid she was going to tell them that she'd let Tom into the house, but she didn't. Grateful beyond words, Glad leaned against the wall she was hiding behind and listened to the rest of the story with horror.

They'd come there to get Judith, Darcy said. And her. Glad had only let them in because Paddy had called and said that he'd had some money for them. And Jessie thought maybe they could work things out so that he'd visit the children. She had insisted that she let them in. The fact that Paddy was bringing his lawyer so that they could sign off on the papers that said he'd be giving them money every week was something they had both agreed would be a good thing.

They needed the money. They were living only on hers and Jessie's Social Security and it wasn't much. Judith had a little saved, but the divorce had cost her plenty.

Darcy sitting next to her on the couch and watching her brothers and sister startled Glad and brought her from her horrible memories. Darcy was mute for several minutes. When she finally spoke to her, it was in low, hushed tones.

"He wasn't telling us the truth. He never did. Did he?"

Glad could have pretended that she didn't know who she was talking about, but it would have been a lie. There were enough of those going around right now and she decided to answer her question. "No. I didn't mean to let him hurt you, Darcy. I swear it. I let him in because he said that he had seen the errors of his ways. And when I left, I didn't know what he was going to do to you." Glad wiped at the tears as she continued. "He's always been only out for himself. Always. I don't know what to tell you, but I swear that I didn't—"

"I know that, Aunt Glad," she told her, cutting her off. "He said once that he didn't know why he married Mom. He thought it was because she didn't want him when he was growing up. Why would he want someone that didn't want him?"

Glad didn't know the answer to that either other than to say Paddy had always been a spoiled brat, so she said nothing. As they sat there watching Sis play with her dollies and the boys try to run them over with their trucks, Glad thought of something else. "How did she save you?"

Darcy looked at her with a frown.

"Your Aunt Alexis, how did she save you? Gordon told me that you said Alexis saved you, but he didn't say how. He said you told him yesterday when you were talking to him and Dallas. You said that she saved your life. How?"

She was so quiet that Glad was sure she wasn't going to answer. Then when she did, she knew that Darcy wasn't telling her everything. She didn't know why she thought so, but she got the feeling that Darcy was protecting her aunt even now…or she still didn't trust her.

"I don't know. I think she put a blanket over me and stopped the pain. I guess the blood that was on me was…it must have been Mom's and not mine like I thought." She looked at Glad then and smiled that sort of half-smile. "You know that's what I meant, don't you?"

Glad nodded and didn't say anything. There were things going on that she didn't understand. They'd all known that Alexis was different, and after Judith died it had become more apparent that whatever she was, she was keeping it to herself. Glad wondered what else she didn't know about her niece. She left the children to go into the other room, her thoughts a jumble of everything.

The kitchen was her solitude. Glad began pulling out things to make some cookies without thinking about what she was doing. Her mind was a muddle of things that were really nothing she could narrow down, so she baked. By the time she'd gotten the batter mixed up and the first sheet of cookies in the oven, she finally came upon the note that Alexis left.

*"I'm at the building making stuff for the shop. Please call me if you need me as I'll have the phone near me. Gordon and his brother may be in and out. I don't know what they're doing, but let them have free rein. A."*

Glad looked out the kitchen window and saw that there were lights on in the building and that some of the doors and windows were open. Smiling, she wondered what sort of concoction Alexis was brewing up now, and she went about her baking. It was several hours and several batches of cookies later when Gordon and Dallas showed up.

~~~

Gordon could smell the other wolf as soon as he walked along the driveway. He knew that it was the same one that had attacked him, and was very careful where he walked. He wanted his brother to get the scent too. After the two of them walked around where Paddy had been they went back up to the house and sat in the kitchen while Gladys filled a plate of cookies for them both.

"What do you think we can do to improve the way this place is locked down?" Gordon looked up at his brother as he shoved two warm chocolate chip cookies in his mouth. "This place has a better security system than we have. Not to mention all the power running through those lines. Who the hell is she trying to keep out?"

Gordon hadn't told Dallas about the other wolf. He wanted him to come there and see for himself what they were dealing with. It made him feel better knowing that the place was secure, but he still had a feeling he was missing something.

"Oh, he's a horror of a man. Why just before they divorced, he threatened me," Jessie said as she entered the room and before Gordon could talk around his cookies. "The nerve of the little pisser. I'll have you know that in my day I could shoot the eye out of a rat."

Gladys huffed. "Last week it was a knife. Get your stories straight, you old bat. And as far as I know, you've never even had a gun in your hands."

"I did too. Last fall when we had that turkey shoot. Remember? You said that I couldn't hit the broad side of a house and I proved I could."

"You did hit the broad side of the house. Nearly shot Alexis in the process. She told you if you ever picked up a gun again she was going to shoot you with it herself." Gladys took a gallon of milk out of the refrigerator and set it between Gordon and Dallas as she continued berating her friend. "And it wasn't a turkey shoot you were at, it was the backyard where Alexis was trying to show us how not to use a gun. You failed. Miserably."

Jessie looked crestfallen for about half a minute then brightened. "Yes. I remember now. I did show her I could load a gun quickly. She was very impressed with that." She took the milk from them and then handed them both a beer.

Gladys took the beers, put them back, and handed them both a glass of milk. "Beer and cookies will make you sick. And yes, she was impressed with your ability to load a gun. But if you remember correctly, which you never do, she told you that she was impressed that you could load a gun so quickly with all the ammo that had already been used. It does little good to have a well-loaded gun if all the bullets in it are already fired. You dolt. I swear you get nuttier every day."

Gordon didn't know how much longer the bickering might have gone on, but the children came into the kitchen at that moment and defused it. They were given milk and cookies too, and after a kiss to both aunts and a hug to both him and Dallas they were sent on their way into the backyard. Dallas grinned at him when the door closed behind them.

"You ready for a family? Seems they've taken to you all right." Dallas picked up another cookie and took a healthy bite. "I'm going to be the favorite uncle and enjoy spoiling them all very soon."

Every wolf that came near him knew that he was claimed and that he had a mate. Gordon's cock jerked in his pants every time he thought of his mate and what they'd done in the forest last night. Christ, she was wonderful, and he found himself wondering where she was right now and if he could go and find her. He looked up when the back door opened and there she stood. His wolf snarled for a taste of her too.

Dallas's laughter brought him back or he might have simply pressed her against the wall and taken her, damn the people around them. He flushed and glanced back at Alexis, whose cheeks were red.

"Down, you two, or we'll never get this finished." Dallas got up, led Alexis to his chair, and then stood next to the counter. "The house is secure. There isn't anything I think we can add to make it any better. The building out back, is it just as locked up?"

Alexis nodded and turned toward Dallas. Gordon felt his breath swoosh from his lungs. Damn it, he felt like he had a constant hard-on around her and wondered if they would ever get enough of each other. Then he grinned. He certainly hoped not.

"I've had several different people work on the system since we moved in. There are four...no, five different alarm companies that have us online, as well as Dark Treasures in town. If someone so much as breathes on the door, the police will be there in seconds." Alexis started to continue, but Gladys chimed in.

"There are also buttons all over the building to press if we are in trouble and open. Alexis showed us where they were and even gave us both a map so we didn't forget where in case somebody comes in." She pulled her map out and handed it to him. "There are a whole bunch of them in the front and a bunch in the back. She even put one in the bathrooms in case we're using the facilities when we get the call."

"We're not to push it if we need toilet paper and we're in there, though. The police were not amused when they busted in the door for that one." Jessie shook her head. "Nope, not one bit. I've had to do some pretty long community service for that one."

Gordon didn't even ask. Being on the force, he had heard about someone calling for help and it turning out to be nothing but a paper run, but he'd never heard it had been Jessie. He was going to call his brother Connor when he got some time and see if he had much information on it. Gordon could see that Dallas wanted to ask, but didn't.

With a shake of his head, Dallas continued. "I want to be able to have a look around the shop if you don't mind. When do you open for business?"

"I have to run some supplies in today. We're normally closed on Sunday and Monday. That's when I go in and replenish what we've sold through the week." Alexis got up and moved toward the door. "I'll let you know when I'm packed up. The van is nearly loaded now and I shouldn't be much longer."

When she went out the door, he stood to follow her. Dallas stopped him with a hand on his chest. The older women left the kitchen about the same time and they could hear their voices fade as they walked away.

"The wolf, do you think he'll try and get to the children? They go back to school tomorrow, right?"

"Yes," he answered Dallas. "I've already made arrangements to have one of the pack pick them up here and take them. They'll also bring them back at the end of the day. There are five teachers there that Austin has told to watch out for them and to protect them as well. Why?"

"Don't know, but I have a feeling that…well, I have something on my mind that I'd like to talk to you about when we're alone." Dallas looked at the door that Gladys and Jessie had gone through. "Do you think the other woman…Jessie…do you think she's as dumb as she appears?"

Gordon started to say she wasn't dumb just confused, but then he realized what his brother was asking. He too looked at the door. Could she be? The two women had been together since the beginning of this and neither of them seemed surprised by Jessie's behavior. Nor did it seem forced or an act. But still, he didn't know for sure.

"What are you asking me? If I think this is a scam and she's a part of it?" He had lowered his voice to nearly nothing, but he knew that his brother would hear him. "You think she's in on whatever is going on here?"

"I don't know," Dallas answered just as quietly. "But I can't believe that she's that stupid about things."

Gordon hadn't thought of it like that. He'd just thought they were funny together. He would wonder now and that was probably why Dallas had told him. He'd keep an eye on both women from now on. He moved toward the door again and out. Dallas said he'd be walking the perimeter again and would wait for the two of them.

KATHI S. BARTON

# CHAPTER 13

Alexis was just putting the last of the barred soap in the box when the door opened behind her. She looked up at Gordon, but didn't stop what she was doing. She was suddenly very nervous around him and shy.

"You should have waited for me to load those boxes in the van for you. They look heavy."

She almost snapped at him that she was fine, but didn't. It wasn't his fault she was in a crappy mood.

"Alexis, what is it?"

"Nothing. I have to get these soaps out now. Those over there weren't ready to wrap yet so I'll have to take them down lat—"

He turned her around, took the bars out of her hand, and set them back on the counter. She looked up at him and bit her tongue so that she wouldn't say anything. He pressed her against the counter and she growled. His smile pissed her off for some reason. Before she could tell him off, he started talking in that low sexy voice of his.

"You know that as a wolf, I have the ability to smell all sorts of things most people can't." He lowered his head to her neck and she nearly moaned. "Like I can smell that you're angry. At what, I can only guess. Like I'm thinking you're pissed because I didn't make love to you this morning before you left the bed."

That wasn't it, but she was beginning to see why that might have been a good reason not to have come down here so early. Making love with this man was worth having a few less things in the store. But she still tried to hold onto her anger.

"I had things to do, and lazing about in the bed with you wasn't going to get things done. I have to support this family, and having you around isn't going to change that." She felt him laugh against her neck. She grabbed a handful of his hair and jerked him away. "This isn't funny, you overgrown pup. I'm pissed at you."

"So I can tell." She was beginning to hate that calmness of his. "Why don't you let go of my hair and tell me what I did to make you so mad at me?"

She let go, but only turned away and started to load the product again. He didn't move and she could feel his heat as he brushed against her several times. She was nearly ready to tell him to get the fuck away from her when he pressed his hard cock into her ass. She stilled when he wrapped his hands around her waist to hold her.

"I want you. I've yet to take you this way, bent over something and me taking you from behind. I want to fuck you this way until you scream out my name. Then I want to turn you around and fuck you again with your ass sitting up on this counter." He rocked into her again. "Christ, I need to be buried deep inside of you."

Before she could stop herself, she was moving against him. Her pussy was already clenching with need of him, and when he growled she knew that he was going to do just what he'd said. After reaching around her, unsnapping her pants, and pulling the zipper nearly out of her jeans, he jerked them down around her hips, then to her knees. She bent over to take them the rest of the way off when he turned her around and sat her on the counter, shoving everything out of his way.

With another growl her pants were off and so was her blouse and bra. She was naked in seconds. He didn't move, didn't touch her for several more, and she wondered what he was going to do. Without a word, he pulled her to her feet and turned her around. She braced both hands on the counter when he put them there and moved her feet back where he positioned her.

"This is going to be quick and hard. I can smell you're wet." His cock pulsed at her entrance and she moaned. "There's no one around us, baby, so I want you to scream when you come. Scream loud and hard."

His cock entered her hard and she pressed back. He wrapped his hand in her hair and pressed her down against the counter before he started fucking her. Her first climax tore through her and her second one caught her in mid scream. He was slamming her hard from behind and she couldn't seem to get enough. When he slid his fingers down her belly and into her pussy, she closed her hand over his and showed him where to touch her.

"Fuck, you're wet. Come again for me Alexis. Flood my hand with your cum and I'll fill you with mine." He pinched her clit hard and she screamed again.

Her voice was raw and she was sure she was going to pass out when he suddenly stiffened and then roared out his own release. His teeth bit into her shoulder hard as he filled her. When he released her shoulder his howl echoed in the room, and she slid into a darkness that felt like home to her.

She was on the couch in her office when she woke. Her clothes were folded neatly with her shoes on top of them when she looked down. Smiling, she threw off the small blanket and started to pull on her panties when she realized she wasn't alone. Gordon was sitting in the chair watching her.

"Did I hurt you?" She shook her head at his question. "I could have. I'm sorry about treating you that way."

"Why? I said you didn't hurt me and I'm reasonably sure that you could hear how much I enjoyed it." She frowned at him. "What's happened?"

He got up, handed her her clothes, and sat down next to her. She started pulling on the rest of her clothes, not sure what else to say. When he spoke, she wished she'd just loaded the van herself and stayed in town.

"Your brother-in-law has been hanging around the property. I've found his scent as close as the gate and a little beyond." He got up and started to pace. "I can't hurt him until he does something that will warrant it. Our laws, pack laws, are older than most human laws."

She looked around the room and thought about her sister and what she'd seen done to her. Alexis looked up at him when he stood by the windows, the sunlight streaming in from around him.

"I'm going to tell you what I've never told anyone else before. It's what happened at the house the day Judith was killed." She moved to the arm of the big sofa and stared at the floor. She didn't think she could look at him and tell him what she'd done. "I'd gotten a call from Judith the week before. She said that she thought something had happened to Paddy and that she was suddenly afraid for her children. He had visitation rights, you see, and she didn't want to hand them over to him any longer."

"Alexis, if you're going to tell me someone else killed your sister, I already know most of it. Darcy told me last night."

She nodded. Darcy had told her that she'd talked to the men. But she needed to tell him everything. "Yes. There was another man there. Tom Garrison was his name. He was there because Paddy had told Aunt Glad that he was his lawyer. When they got there, Paddy lost control. His...monster sort of came forth and attacked. But he didn't get far. He only got as far as hitting Judith."

"You were there? I thought Darcy said you'd shown up later?" She nodded. "When is it that you came to the house?"

"That morning. I was there because I was helping them pack up. Darcy was sick and Sis was playing in her room. I'd heard the shouting and came down after locking Sis in her closet and calling the police." She wiped at the tears she didn't know had been falling. "Paddy was on the floor and he was a wolf. He'd been tranquilized by something strong. Tom had shot him with his cane just as I came into the room. It was already too late to save Judith."

He sat on the floor in front of her, took her chin in his hand, and brought her face to his. No matter how hard she tried, she couldn't pull away. He kissed her gently on the mouth before he spoke.

"You tried to save her, didn't you? That's why you didn't want to help me. You were afraid of failing again, weren't you?" She nodded as he continued. "Did you.... Honey, did you try to kill Tom? At any time, did you try to kill him?"

She pulled away this time and he let her. She wasn't sure why he had, but was more grateful than she'd ever been about anything. She shook her head before she told him what she'd done. "I had a brief moment of murderous hatred and that was all. He'd already killed Judith, as I've said, but Darcy was...she was nearly dead too. I had to save her, and if I had killed him, then she would have died too." She looked at him now. "You understand, don't you? I couldn't let her die. She was my sister's child."

"Yes, love, you had to save her. And I'm very proud of you for doing so. Darcy will be all right soon, you'll see. You did just what you had to do."

She nodded and looked away. "But I wanted him dead. And every day I think about killing him, making him pay for what he did to my sister and her child. I'm a horrible person for wanting to see him suffer, suffer for everything he did."

~~~

Gordon was still sitting in the office when his brother came in. He glanced up at Connor, but didn't speak. He decided to ignore him when Connor sat in the chair across from him and said nothing. He had a lot to deal with and conversation wasn't going to help. When Austin and

Dallas came in a few minutes later he knew that someone had told them that he was upset.

"I'm fine. Really, I am. I have a lot to think about and I'm just going to sort it out, then I'll go and find Alexis and we'll talk." He hoped so anyway. She'd been so quiet when she'd left him that he wasn't sure what they'd said after she told him what she'd done.

"Okay, but you might want to take a look at the clock, buddy. You've been sitting here for over four hours." He looked over at Connor, sure he was kidding. "You were supposed to meet us at the shop over three hours ago. Good thing your mate is a bit more punctual than you are."

"Alexis," he said as he stood. Christ, he'd forgotten to go with her to keep her safe. He was nearly to the door when Austin stopped him.

"She's in the kitchen with CJ. They're arguing over dinner plans...something about eating a frozen pizza over ordering Chinese. It seems neither of our mates can cook worth a damn."

Gordon sat back down and looked at his family. He didn't know where to begin. Not to mention he didn't think they'd believe him anyway...hell, he didn't believe it either. As he got up again and poured himself a drink, he tried to think. Gordon rarely drank, but felt that now would be a good time to start. Downing the hard liquor, he sat back down. It was still burning his throat when he started talking.

"Alexis said I could let you know what she's done." He looked around again. "Christ, she's amazing."

Austin grinned. "You should know that we are already in agreement with you there. She's your mate so she already has our support. If she can twist you up like this, then she has another point in her favor."

Gordon knew what his brother was doing. He was trying to make it easier on him to say whatever he thought he needed to tell them. He wasn't worried that they'd hurt his mate. They wouldn't do that, but they might ask them to leave, which he really couldn't blame them for once they heard what he had.

"Alexis has known for a while that she is different. Hell, not just different, but fucking different." He took a deep breath before starting over. "She saved me, as you know, but she also healed her niece. She can...she can heal people. Not just heal them, but nearly bring them back from the dead heal them. "

"We know that, buddy. When she saved you, you were all but dead. So what is it you think we don't know?" Connor asked him. "Has Phil told you anything more about what he thinks she is? Is that it...you know what she is and you're afraid we'll reject her for it?"

Gordon knew his brother was smart and he smiled when he got it so quickly. "No. He's still not talking to me. But I'm working on something that will hopefully get me on his better side. At least, I hope it does. And I'm not afraid you're going to reject her, but she is. And I'm having a hard time trying to convince her of it."

"Of course she would. She hasn't had a great deal of reason to trust any of us so far, but we're working on that. She's a hell of a woman." Austin frowned before he continued. "Is she worried that we're going to put her brother-in-law down? The council has already said he must die. Once a were kills, especially the way that Patrick did, they feel there is no redeeming hope for them. I'm working on trying to get him a stay, but you know how they can be."

Yes, he did know. And Gordon hated to admit it, but he felt that after what he'd done to his ex-wife and daughter, Gordon didn't want him around either. He'd be up to something all the time and he'd be a shadow in their lives.

"No. I think that bothers her as much as it worries her. She wants both men out of her life. And the children's. She has custody of them, did I mention that?" He got up to go to the bar again and decided he didn't need it. "I love those kids as much as if they were my own. I can't let him hurt them again. Not ever. I have to do everything in my power to protect them. But she…."

"She what?" Austin asked. "She won't let you? She doesn't trust you?" Gordon nodded, agreeing to all the questions. "I see. Then we'll just have to show her what we can do."

He knew that they'd help him, but that wasn't the problem. The problem was he wanted to show her he could do it. But he knew that with what was going on, he'd more than likely end up getting someone killed or hurt, and he didn't want that either. He knew them all well enough to know that they'd have a million questions, but they'd think them out. They were all alphas, had been born that way. Someday they'd all lead their own packs, and this was what would make them great leaders.

"So you're saying that she doesn't want your help or that she is telling you to fuck off?" Gordon nodded at Dallas's question. "Oh, I like this one. She can not only twist you up, but make you question your manliness too. Yeah, I really like her."

"Fuck you. And that's not all. The healing thing? She can control when her touch is needed and how she is to use it, but if she heals a person, that person has a small bit of her. Not a lot, just enough to heal them and maybe…and it doesn't happen often…maybe they can heal something too. But it will be on a very small scale. Like a plant or maybe a scratch." Gordon showed them the cut on his leg. "If you guys would have looked, she told me you would have seen the same cut on her leg."

Austin suddenly looked up. "Did she tell you what she took from you?"

She had. That's what he'd been thinking about all this time. What he'd given her and what…and what she'd given him. He started to pace again, knowing that this was going to be the turning point. His race just didn't like what his mate was.

"She is my mate, but I'm hers as well. When we mated and bonded…well, it was a two-way thing. I'm not sure I understand all of it, but basically, we're now a part of each other." He rolled his neck and didn't look at his brother as he continued. "She can shift into a wolf. She can shift into anything she wants. Alexis is a shifter."

Austin was very quiet. Gordon didn't look at him as he walked to the desk and leaned against it. He was actually excited, but also afraid. Wolf packs generally disliked shifters for several reasons. The most important reason was that they somehow messed with the balance of things. Gordon wasn't sure how, but he'd been hearing that since he'd been a small cub.

Austin nodded. "Let me get this straight. You think…or she thinks…that because she's a shifter, we're somehow going to shun you and her? Am I right?" Gordon nodded, knowing that it sounded really stupid now that someone had said it out loud. "Of all the…and what did you tell her? That it was a part of our history to do that, or did she read about it in some stupid fairy tale book?"

"Book. But she's right. We do shun shifters and any weres that mate with them. I've heard—"

"Oh for the love of…are you listening to yourself? Shun her? Christ, do you have any idea what CJ would do to you if she even had a hint of what you were thinking? You'd better not tell her what we've talked about. She'll run your nuts up the flagpole and set fire to them. Christ." Austin grinned. "I just might tell her to see what you'll do to try and win her back to your side."

Every man in the room held himself. CJ could be a tad vicious and since she'd been pregnant, she'd been a little more aggressive. Their mom said it was natural, she was an alpha. Gordon grimaced at his brother, wondering what he'd have to do to keep him from telling her.

"You keep my secret and I'll keep yours." Gordon didn't really know anything, but the threat seemed to work. Before his brother figured out he was bluffing, he'd have to think hard on something worthy of not getting castrated. Gordon was sure he could think of something, but right now he was a little busy trying to keep his new family safe.

Austin backed away from him and sat down. He didn't comment on the threat, but simply nodded toward him. Gordon moved over to the chair again and sat down. He was sure his brother would talk to him later about it.

"Have you talked to Phil?"

Gordon shook his head, knowing his brother was trying to change the subject.

"I want this resolved between the two of you by the next full moon. You fucked up and you're going to do whatever it takes to fix this. He's a good friend to our pack and CJ is upset that he won't come around."

Gordon nodded. "I will. I've been...he won't answer my calls. I've left him several messages and—"

"Then go to his house. Fix this, Gordon, or I will fix you. Do you understand me? I want this resolved. Now." Austin stood. "Now, as for you and your mate...I'm sure you expect me to be pissy or something, but I'm not. I'm actually thrilled for you both. I can't wait to see her wolf. Has she shifted into one yet?"

"Yes, she's silver. She's sort of afraid of her, though. She's never shifted to wolf before. And she's a little overwhelmed by all this. Well, there is the brother-in-law thing. I've told her that he's hanging around her place. I don't think she is taking this part of him seriously. She seems to think she can handle him."

Austin nodded. "Maybe she can. I wouldn't underestimate her. I'll be the first to admit that women, especially mates, are much stronger than we give them credit for." Austin moved to the door. "And if you tell CJ I said that, I'll hunt you down and cut your nuts off myself."

Gordon was still laughing when he got into his truck to drive into town after dinner. Alexis had gone in before him with Dallas. Her shop was brightly lit and he could see her moving around inside. He was nearly out of the vehicle when he saw someone hiding in the alleyway. His cell phone going off startled him.

"Don't go near him. If you do, then I won't get him to return," Alexis said before he could say anything. "Just come inside if you're going to, but don't pay any attention to the boy."

Against his better judgment, Gordon got out of his truck and walked past the kid trying to hide against the building. Gordon did take a deep breath and nearly stopped to check the wolf out, but didn't. He went inside when Alexis opened the door and pulled her into his arms.

"Your boy is a girl," he whispered in her ear. "And she's a wolf, did you know that?"

# CHAPTER 14

Phil listened to the message again. It's not that he wanted to talk to Gordon, but the message from CJ made him think he'd better or else. He had to smile at that. Here he was a four hundred-year-old vampire and he was afraid of one little wolf who was barely out of her training period. Phil picked up his phone to call her.

"I have some papers you need to come by and sign off on. And the property on Main Street is now yours if you still want it." He smiled when she didn't answer right away. "Of course if you don't want it any more I'm sure I can find any number of buyers for it."

"You are so full of shit it's not funny. And if you try and sell that property I'll hunt you down and rip your fangs out." She laughed. "This is not going to get you out of what I asked you to do."

He didn't think it would work, but he had to try. "Are you sure? Because from where I'm sitting, not talking to your brother-in-law is getting me all sorts of work done. If I have to answer his calls or even call him back it's going to put me way behind and frankly, my dear, I could care less how sorry he is."

That wasn't entirely true. Phil missed the cop. Gordon had been very helpful to him when he'd needed it. Gordon had given him more information on things Phil knew he shouldn't have known about to help him out in a couple of other things he'd had going on. Phil looked over at the framed picture of the entire family and of him and Gordon standing next to each other with their arms around each other at CJ's and Austin's wedding. Pain had him looking away and he nearly missed what CJ was saying.

"What do you mean he needs me more than ever? What the hell has he done now?" Phil sat up and punched a few keys on his computer to bring up the local newspaper. "I don't see in the paper where he's murdered anyone."

CJ laughed and he felt marginally better. "No, you dork. I want you to talk to him about Alexis. She told him she's a shifter. Well, she told him she could change into any animal she wanted and he surmised she's a shifter. There is something else, too, but I don't understand it. Something to do with pack law."

Pack law. Those two words excited and terrified him at the same time. He thought about what his mother had told him about Strongs. They were immortals once, but over the centuries things had changed. They sort of bred out the fact that they could live forever. He picked up the leather bound book that his mother had given him.

"I can help him from here. I have a book that he can read. It's very informative and—"

"I swear to Christ, if you make me come over there, I'm going to...I'm going to pee on your very ugly, expensive carpet. Then I might rub your nose in it." She huffed and he laughed...to himself. He wasn't stupid. "Come over, please. I miss you, and since you're avoiding him I don't get to see you. And he does need you. He needs you almost as much as I do."

Phil rubbed the sudden pain over his heart. Holy Christ, he loved her. And he had loved her from the very beginning, but not romantically, never that. Phil leaned back in his chair and closed his eyes. He knew he was going to regret this, but he would do anything for CJ and she knew it.

"All right. I'll come over to your house, but not his. And he'll keep any comments to himself or so help me I'll never come to you again. Understand?" She said she did. "And I want something from him. I want to know where to find Holly. It's high time she and I figure this shit out between us or cut our ties."

"I don't know where she is, but if he does I'll make him understand that he has to give you the information. And Phil?" He waited for her to continue, but she only waited.

"Yes, love. What is it?" He closed his eyes again when she laughed that small laugh he'd come to love about her.

"I think you should know that you're my very best friend, and I doubt that I'll ever have anyone I love like I do you."

She hung up before he could form an answer. He gently put the phone on his desk and looked around the office. He could have been anywhere in the world...had been, actually, before meeting her. Now, here he was, stuck in the middle of nowhere, in a job he sort of liked, but was very good at, and his mate was who knew where.

151

He stood up and picked up the book his mother had given him. Time to go and see what he could tell the others about what he'd learned. He only hoped that he didn't have to murder the wolf before he let him know that he was going to live forever. He also hoped that when he told the man…and the girl…that they took the news better than his mother had.

"What do you mean she isn't human? That is no answer, young man. I want you to tell me what makes you believe she's any more than…well, any more than what she appears." His mother had gotten on the phone when Phil had asked his dad what he knew about the legend of shifters.

He took a deep breath and let it out slowly. "She can heal with a touch and…." This was the hard part. "She can heal all supernaturals, including wolves."

He'd been told all his life that wolves, werewolves to be exact, were the hardest, if not impossible, animals to heal. If they couldn't shift and heal, or heal on their own, then they were dead. It was the natural way of things. But he'd been there when she'd healed Gordon, and knew that the man had taken his last breath and his heart had beat for the last time when Alexis touched him.

His mother had been quiet for so long that he was sure she had hung up and was now at his front door, but she'd spoken slowly and very quietly after a bit.

"What makes you think of a shifter, son? I mean, she could simply be a witch and has the power to do so." He knew she didn't want to believe it. Hell, he'd not wanted to believe it either. "Could you be wrong? Have you...Christ, please tell me you haven't tasted her blood without permission."

"No," he assured her. "I've not tasted her. I've asked and so far have been told no. But, well, Mom, I'm nearly as positive as I can be about this. She is a shifter as surely as you're my mother."

He'd hoped to make her laugh and, if failing that, to lighten the situation, but she'd either been too upset or simply overwhelmed, he wasn't sure which. But what she said next scared him enough that he'd gone to their home and picked up the book she'd told him he could have.

"That poor girl. What is she going to do now? The wolf pack won't accept her now, will they? And that poor man. What will he do, not being able to take his mate?"

He nodded. "I know, Mom. But...well, I don't think she knows what they could do to her, unless one of them has told her. She's very brave and strong. I just...Mom, I really like this girl. I do need to tell her, tell her everything so that we can deal with this and her one step at a time."

"I have a book. It's been in our family since my mother's mother was born. I'll send it to you and you.... Christ, have her read it, and if one of those stupid dogs hurts her, hurts even one hair on her head, you tell them that I will hunt them down and drain them."

With tears in his eyes, he hung up after assuring her he would. As he had closed his phone he did something he'd not done for decades. Phil prayed. He had done it several times since his conversation, and also since he'd read the book. It was a very terrifying story and he didn't like the things it had to say about his kind.

Alexis Dark Force was an oddity that even he, in all his years walking the earth, had never seen. Phil had never even heard of one, a pure one, existing any more.

~~~

Tom watched the wolf pace. He liked it when Paddy came to visit. If he could only let him drink from him then things would be so much better. But Paddy wasn't very trusting. Not that Tom could really blame him. He'd been a bit over the top about a few things, one of them being the ex-wife.

"I want you to sit. Why you think that I relish having the carpet cleaned after you get your fur all over it is beyond me." Tom smiled when Paddy did just what he'd told him to do with a small whimper. "You can shift if you bothered to bring yourself other clothes. I do not want a naked man in my house any more than I want fur all over the place."

The shift was sudden and that startled Tom. He'd seen wolves shift before. It was a long and messy process and he'd been sickened by it. But Paddy had gone from canine to human in less than a handful of seconds. He tried to act as if he wasn't impressed, but he wasn't sure that Paddy had believed him, and that made him sharper than he'd meant to be.

"Oh for the love of Christ, will you please get dressed?" He hadn't realized that in his musings he'd missed the man dressing. "Sit over there and try not to break anything. There are things in this room worth more than you make in several lifetimes."

Paddy had looked at him like he was confused, but said nothing as he sat in one of the oldest chairs in the room. Tom didn't collect antiques for their value like most people, or even for the fact that they were from a time gone by. No, he collected them because someone else had wanted them...or had owned them. He didn't care what he'd had to do to get them so long as the other person didn't get whatever it was.

He'd been doing things like this, buying or stealing—well, mostly stealing—since he'd been told by his mother that he couldn't have the bike next door because Ronnie's parents had purchased the last one like it. It had only taken him one day to figure out that she'd lied, but by then he'd already stolen the bike and sold it to a kid on another block for a tidy amount. When confronted, Tom had confessed and had gotten a good beating, but all he'd learned from it was that the next time he stole something for a profit he was not to get caught. He'd not been caught since.

"Alexis said that I can't come on the property any more. She has a restraining order against me and if I break it, I'll end up in jail. I'm not going back to jail, not for anything." Paddy looked down after he'd spoken. "I just don't like prison. They don't treat you right in there."

Tom sighed. "Of course they don't, you moron. If they did, it would be called a vacation and you'd be expected to tip them. I think it's sort of expected for them to treat you badly." He handed a file to Paddy as he continued. "These are the specs on the alarm system in the house. The most important one is the gate. You should be able to follow those instructions to the letter, am I correct?"

Tom didn't think that Paddy could follow directions on a paper bag to open it, but didn't say it. Since he'd been working with this idiot on getting Alexis Dark he'd been more surprised than anything that he'd not been caught or killed. Patrick Booth was by far the stupidest man he'd ever met.

"I can do it." Paddy looked over the pages, but Tom had already figured out that he didn't have a clue what it was. "Where'd you get this stuff anyway? I thought it was against the law to give this out if you were the one who put it in."

*Duh*, Tom wanted to shout at him. "I have an inside source. And before you ask, no, I'm not going to tell you who it is. Suffice it to say that my contact has been working with me for some time."

And she had too. He wondered why she hadn't been caught either. He would have thought that someone like Alexis Dark would have caught onto her some time ago. He would have. The woman was a fool if she didn't think that someone from that pack, one of the men who guarded their alpha, would figure her out soon enough.

"When you want me to go and get her? And where do you want me to bring her once I get her?" Tom nearly smiled again. Paddy was making it sound like now that he had the codes to get inside the residence the people in the house were going to be so impressed that they'd simply go where he wanted. "I should also have a car or something to drive her around in. The police took my other one when they raided my house. Stupid fuckers think I murdered somebody."

Tom nodded. He didn't doubt for a moment that Paddy had killed someone, probably a few someones. But he only nodded sardonically at the wolf.

"Sure. And let me make sure that I drive you there too." Paddy started to nod, but stopped when he realized that Tom wasn't being serious. This man was going to get himself dead. And very soon.

"I'll go down there today and try and snatch her out tonight. All right?" Tom didn't as much as move his fingers in answer to his question. "I'll get her for you. You don't have to worry."

After Paddy left Tom picked up the phone. As it rang on the other end, he thought about having Alexis Dark for one night. The woman was going to be begging him if it was the last thing she did. Even as the phone was being answered he thought it might be the last thing she did. Begging him would make it all the more fulfilling for him.

"Paddy is breaking in today. Kill him." He hung up the phone before his contact in the house could answer. Tom was smiling as he got up and left his office. Things were beginning to look up for him and he thought that by this time Friday he'd be set in all the things he wanted.

He went to his basement. Calling it a basement was an overstatement. He'd had it dug out just after he acquired the house. It was his place of rest...it was also his playroom and his laboratory. He sat in the chair behind the desk in the office that was far superior to the one above him. Not only was the desk bigger, but the equipment and computer system here were much more advanced.

He had a monitoring system that watched over every room in the house and every inch of the yard beyond him. The alarm alone had cost him millions and he thought it well worth it. Birds didn't even land on his grass any more as they were killed instantly when they dared try. The surrounding fence and high barbed wired had kept out everything that thought to scale it. The power that hummed along it was enough to fry even the largest of prey, and when he turned it up to full amperage the place practically sang with energy. This was why Tom rarely left his compound and had his dinner brought to him. Smiling, he switched a few buttons and looked inside the house of Alexis Dark.

The kitchen and the living room were the only two rooms he could see. His partner had been less than helpful when he'd had her install the remotes. But he supposed that she'd done the best she could. Alexis had been on top of every little thing that had gone on inside the renovations to the house. Not that he could blame her. Alexis was a very beautiful and rare woman.

He glanced down at the sheets of paper that had come to him last night, and now he knew just what it was about her that intrigued him so much. Alexis was a shifter. The last of her breed and, even better, full blooded. Now he needed to taste her more than ever. Tom knew without a doubt that her blood would be like a fine wine and a thick steak all at once. He was looking forward to her blood like he did anything expensive he obtained.

Tom watched the play between the people in the room on the monitor screen. The youngest child, he thought her name was simply Sis, was messy and he'd be glad to have her dead. She ate her human food like it was the best thing she'd ever tasted and, to his horror, she showed the person sitting across from her what was in her mouth every few minutes. Tom shuddered. He hated children of all kinds and thought that their only purpose should be to feed his kind. Flipping the switch, he watched the living room.

The girl Darcy sat in there alone. She sat with her head down and her hands in her lap. He wished he knew what was going on in her mind. The girl had frankly creeped him out since the day he'd killed her mother. And as for her being alive, that little bit of information had been a surprise too. He'd thought her dead like the mother. That was another thing he had to thank Alexis for. She'd been responsible for Darcy as well.

The girl continued to sit, and he was about ready to change back to the kitchen in hopes of the little one being gone or to see that she'd choked to death on whatever she'd been eating when Darcy looked up. She didn't look around the room, but simply up. It took him several seconds to realize that she was staring at him.

Tom leaned forward in his chair. He scanned the rest of the room to see if anyone had come into it while he'd been focused on her, but could see that both doorways into the room were clear and that it appeared that no one was with her. When she stood up and walked toward the camera, he held his breath.

Darcy walked right toward him, and when her face was the only thing he could see in his camera view, she puckered her lips and kissed the air. Tom leaped back, swearing that he could feel her lips on his face. When she smiled and turned away Tom let out his pent up breath. When she stopped in the doorway leading to the kitchen, she turned toward him once again and flipped him her middle finger.

Tom found himself staring at the spot where she'd stood for a long time. All that kept rolling around in his mind was that she knew. She knew, she knew, she knew. Reaching over with shaking fingers, he turned off the monitor, something he'd not done since having the camera set up. Terror, a thing he'd not felt for many, many centuries, flushed his skin with sweat. Then the anger set in.

She'd been told. That was the only reason she'd known where the camera was set up. The woman he'd had in the house around them all for decades had told her. For whatever reason she'd told mattered little to him now. Now she had to die. Along with the rest of the humans in the household, his plant had to die.

# CHAPTER 15

Alexis drove to the pack house with Gordon sitting beside her. She was still trying to figure out what the young female wolf had wanted hanging around her shop.

"What do you know about her?" Gordon startled her out of her musings. "The wolf, how long has she been hanging around your shop?"

She tried to remember. "I guess a little over a month now. I didn't know she was a *she* though. And if you tell me that you asked her I'll murder you. I don't know what she wants, but she's only been hanging around, not causing me any problems."

"I could smell her. She's also a virgin, but not a young girl. I would say that she's in her mid-thirties or less, but not much. She should have a mate by now, or at least a pack to be in. She doesn't smell like anything but her. No other males have been near her for some time."

Alexis glared at him. "You got all that by smelling her? Just how close were you to her? I mean, that's a great deal of information for someone who only sniffed the air." She sounded jealous and hated that. When she stopped at

161

the light Gordon leaned over and licked her neck. Every nerve ending in her body went on alert.

"You smell delicious, love. If we weren't commanded to be at the pack house to meet with Phil I'd have you pull over and I'd show you how much I love the way you smell." She sat at the light too long thinking about what he was saying, and the person behind her beeped. Flustered and a little mad, she nearly killed the engine popping the clutch.

"Stop doing that," she told him when she got moving again. "You know that I don't like you very much, and that is so not helping your cause right now. What does Phil want anyway? I thought he was pissed at you still."

He moved back to his side of the car and looked out the window. She had made him mad, but she thought she might be safer if he was mad at her and not trying to have sex with her all the time. When he spoke she felt really bad for what she'd done.

"I hurt him. And in hurting him, I hurt CJ. Now my alpha is pissed and wants me to fix this. I want to as well. I hate having Phil pissed off at me. He's a good friend and what I did and said to him wasn't right." He reached over and took her hand before he continued. "I was afraid and I said some things, some horrible things about his kind, and I have regretted it since. But I think I have a way to fix it. I'm just waiting for—"

The wolf shot in front of them in seconds. If she'd not been looking where she had been going she might have hit it. Jerking the vehicle to a sudden stop made her seatbelt cut into her deeply, but the fear of hurting Gordon overrode the pain until she was sure he was all right. He was staring at the wolf as it stood watching them from the middle of the road.

"Did I hit it?" She started to get out to check when he squeezed her hand. "You know that wolf?"

Without taking his eyes from the wolf, he answered her, and she looked back when he did. "You do as well. It's your female. She wants something. Are you comfortable enough to get out and go to her?"

Was she? Probably not, but she knew that the girl had been hanging around the shop for over a month now and Alexis wanted to help her if she needed her. She unbuckled the belt and slowly opened the door. When Gordon started to open his door the wolf stood up and her fur stood on end. Gordon stopped, but didn't shut the door.

"He's my...well, fuck it, he's my mate. And you know how stupid they can be if you don't do what they think is best for you." Alexis got out as she spoke. "Sometimes I wouldn't mind so much if you ripped him up a bit, but I think that whatever it is you want, he can probably help."

The seconds went by slowly. Alexis wasn't sure if the girl/wolf was going to settle down or if she was going to run. When she lay down but didn't take her eyes off of Gordon, Alexis relaxed a little. She heard the door close behind her and assumed that Gordon had exited on his side.

"How do I talk to her? I mean, unless you can understand barking we're going to have a bit of a problem here." Alexis glanced over at Gordon when he chuckled a little. "This is not the time to make fun of me. I'm serious here. She wants to—"

The voice that echoed in her mind was faint, but still there. She turned to look at the wolf and was surprised that she'd moved closer to them. Alexis put out her hand, but didn't move otherwise. The wolf came up and put her head under Alexis's outstretched hand.

*"I'm Stacy, Stacy O'Brien. If you can hear me, would you please get down on your knees? I won't hurt you."*

"She said her name is Stacy O'Brien. Can you hear her too?" When Gordon didn't answer, she turned to look at him. "Gordon?"

"I can hear her. Alexis, I should explain that you hearing her without being an alpha, her alpha, is very unusual. Have you been able to hear wolf before?" She shook her head at his question. "I can hear her because you can. I think. Hell, who knows?"

*"You're special. And very strong."* Stacy put her head in Alexis's lap when she sat on the road. *"When we touch, I can hear you much better."*

"Why are you running around at night? Are you trying to get killed? My God, I could have run over you." Alexis started to rub her fingers through Stacy's fur and could hear a rumble coming from her. "Gordon said you needed to talk, so talk or come with me to the pack house and we can talk there."

This time, the wolf whimpered before answering. *"The pack won't take me. I'm barren, or so they've told me. I cannot carry on the next generation, so the last pack said I was to be killed. I left there before they could carry out the order."*

Alexis looked at Gordon, who shook his head. "That won't happen to you here. There are plenty of males who've lost their mates and could use a good companion. Come to the pack house and we'll welcome you."

*"The man who comes to harm you, do you know of who I speak?"* Alexis started to say no, but stopped when Stacy continued. *"Not the one who smells like the young pups...children. The older one, the one who smells of blood, old and dirty blood."*

"I know the other man, the one who smells like my nieces and nephews. The other, he's a vampire, I guess?" Stacy whimpered again when Alexis asked. "Okay. Don't know who that is unless it's Phil. Is that who it is?"

*"No. The lawyer smells clean and very fresh, not like this man. He and his kind are what I fear. They like the taste of wolf blood, especially that of a virgin. No, this man wishes you harm, and he smells like one of the older women in your pack."*

Alexis looked up when she heard a car coming. Without thought to what might happen to them, she stood and opened the back door to her vehicle. With a sharp command, Stacy leapt inside and Alexis closed the door, thankful that Gordon had gotten in as well.

They were moving down the road before the car came around the corner. Several times she looked at the wolf in the back as she drove, but the wolf stayed low. Alexis was sure she knew who was behind them because she continued to whimper all the way to the pack house. When they pulled into the gated area, the car, a black SUV, sped by them.

They were moving up the drive before anyone spoke. And when Gordon did Alexis wasn't sure if she wanted to go inside or not. There were things going on that she was sure were going to be bad.

"The persons in the car, they were following us, you know that, right?" She stared at him. "The pack will help us, Alexis, all of us." He looked at the wolf in the back. "All of us."

~~~

Gordon was rolling out of the vehicle before it came to a complete stop. He was glad that he'd reached out to Austin. He was even gladder that they had taken his warning seriously and were now standing on the front deck with about two dozen shifted wolves surrounding CJ, Dallas, and him.

"He drove by, but I got his plate. I don't think it was a coincidence that he just happened on that road at that time. Send a few wolves after him and see if they can pick him up." Alexis was coming around her vehicle with Stacy as the wolves did his bidding. "This is Stacy O'Brien. She'll need something to put on when she—"

"You hold it right there, mister." Gordon turned and raised a brow to Alexis as she snapped at him. "You aren't the big cheese here, and I'm pretty sure the last time I looked, women had all kinds of rights that even big, bad wolves like you can understand."

Gordon heard his brothers laugh and CJ was the loudest. He was about ready to snarl at his mate when she came up to him with her wolf friend standing between them. With a snap of her finger and a sharp point to the right, Stacy moved.

"You did that really well," Austin said with laughter in his voice. "So Gordon, you've found yourself an alpha person and didn't even know it."

Gordon didn't know whether to be pleased or pissed. He opted for pleased with a small dose of pissed when he turned to look at Alexis. Christ, she was beautiful standing there with three wolves standing behind her. Gordon wasn't sure where they'd come from, but he was sure he was gathering a pack without even knowing it. He glanced at the two males and Stacy and then back at Alexis.

"Do you have any idea what Austin is talking about?" He wasn't surprised when she shook her head. "The wolves that are there with you have just pledged themselves and their loyalty to you. By breaking pack from Austin's, we've just inherited them into ours. Understand?"

"I don't want a pack," she said, trying to step away from them, and he noticed that Stacy stayed where she was. "I can barely be parent to a few kids. I can't imagine how it will be trying to be a...I thought it was called an alpha bitch?"

Gordon tried not to laugh, but when CJ came down off the deck and toward them he knew that her explanation was going to be worth it. He watched her waddle toward them, her and all seven months of her belly.

"Oh, I'm so not going to be called a bitch of any kind. When Austin called me that the first time I nearly took his head off." CJ grinned. "Actually, I threatened all sorts of things I was going to do to him, so we came up with 'alpha person.' Though now I suppose that alpha bitch is more suiting. I've been something of a terror these past few months."

The man on the deck didn't say a word…at least not out loud, but Gordon heard him through their brotherly link. *"Something of a terror? Holy hell, she's been a nightmare. And if you tell her I said that, I'll make you a eunuch. All of you."*

"All right. The pack said that they got nothing from the SUV," Dallas said quietly. "We should take this inside. Come. Now."

Gordon watched the pack move as one. The only few that stayed were the two males, the names of which Gordon couldn't remember, and Stacy. She didn't move even though the compulsion was very strong. The only indication she gave that she'd heard him was a small flick of her ear. Gordon tried to hide his laughter behind his hand when Dallas tried again to get them to move.

"Oh for heaven's sake," Alexis said. "Come on in, guys. I think it's going to be a really long night and I, for one, could use a beer."

The males stood and looked back at Stacy, who hadn't moved. When Alexis told him to go inside and take the others with him Gordon started to tell her no, but Stacy growled low in her throat and spoke to him again.

*"I won't go in as a wolf…not here with all those males. I'll talk to Alexis, but not to anyone in the house."* Gordon didn't get a chance to answer her before she spoke again. *"I will protect her. I was the head of security in the other pack. Your mate will be safe with me."*

Gordon looked directly to the female, knowing that Austin and Alexis both would be able to hear him and not caring. "Harm comes to her and I will kill you. I will make it a long and horrible death, so much so that you'll beg for your death."

*"No harm with come to her. None. On this I swear my allegiance to you. I will die, myself, before harm comes to her."*

Gordon nodded. He turned on his heel and entered the house without another backward glance. He knew what he was doing was foolhardy, but he also knew that the female was right. She would die for Alexis. It was the why that puzzled him.

"She won't die. Neither will you." Gordon looked at Phil as he spoke. "Your mate is the last shifter in this world. And boy, have I got a story for you."

Gordon reached out and grabbed the vampire before he could think about it. He pulled his friend into his body and gave him a hug that only other supes could give each other—tight and hardy. When he released him, Phil held on for just a few seconds longer and Gordon felt the weight of the past few days lighten just a little. Before he stepped back, he whispered in Phil's ear.

"She's in New York. She's there on a business trip that will bring her back this way in two weeks. If you want to catch her there she's staying at the Beverly Wilshire on Tenth."

Phil stepped back. The look of shock on his face was priceless. Before either of them said a word, though, Gordon's mother came from the kitchen. She was holding a tray of food and both men reached to take it from her.

"No, I have it. Come on. I have a bag of clothes on the table for the young girl. CJ said she needed something to put on." She set the tray down as she started handing out sandwiches. "There are some bigger shirts and a few of those stretchy pants too. Not sure how big she is, but I'm thinking she's a tiny little thing. The children are in the back yard playing with some of the other pack, and your Aunt Glad is having herself a lay in. Poor thing is all done in. Gordon, your brother said he would be by later. He said to tell you he's on a case and you'd understand. Come on now, let's begin. I'm dying to know what this pretty book is about."

They adjourned to the living room as CJ took the bag of clothing out to the deck. She was gone for awhile, and when Gordon started to get up to see if anything had happened to Alexis, Austin stopped him with a hand on his arm.

"They're fine. The pack is watching them. And your pack is still on the steps. By the way, congratulations are in order, I suppose. Those two...." Austin nodded to the front door and the two males sitting there watching. "They've been uncomfortable here for a few months and were just about to move on. I'm glad they found you and Alexis."

Gordon only nodded. He'd not only gotten a mate, it seemed, but a pack as well. He wondered where they'd go from there, and wondered if they could stay at least for a little while longer. He didn't want to leave his family just yet, especially not with Austin becoming a father in a few months. He nodded again before he took a healthy bite from the sandwich and a good drink of iced tea. As much as he wanted a beer, he wasn't sure what was going on outside and wanted to be on his best game.

He looked up when CJ and Alexis came in with a very beautiful woman. He stood up and started toward her. He'd only seen her from afar, but the scent was all hers. He was nearly to her when she snarled deep in her throat at him. This woman had claws.

"Gordon, I'd stay back if I were you. She's a tad touchy about being in here and you're making her hackles rise."

He glanced at Alexis then back at the girl. "She will learn her place or leave."

Stacy started to turn away when Alexis grabbed her arm. It happened so quickly that Gordon had very little time to get back, but Alexis caught the worst of it.

Stacy's claws were suddenly at Alexis before he could move her. The blood splattered on his face and body as they tore into her flesh. All Gordon could do was grab onto Alexis as she started to slide to the floor. As he set her down as gently as he could and tried to stop the blood, he heard the fight behind him. It wasn't until someone shouted that all noise stopped.

# CHAPTER 16

"Gordon, let her go. You have to let her go so that she can heal."

Gordon looked up at him and Phil was sure he was only half hearing him. "Let Alexis go. The healing will begin as soon as you stop touching her. She won't die. I promise you, she won't die."

"She cut her. She killed her...Phil, I can't lose her. I love her very much." Gordon looked down at her again before Phil could get him away. "I can't. I love her."

"Her body needs to heal. Just don't touch her and she'll heal." Phil glanced at the wound. "Look, Gordon. See, her wound is closing and she's stopped bleeding. If you let her go, she'll heal faster."

Phil wasn't sure if Gordon staggered back or simply let her go, but Alexis was suddenly healing much faster. They all stood and watched as her skin healed over and became flawless. When she suddenly took in a deep breath, at that moment he realized she'd not been breathing. Her eyes opening startled him as well.

"They're silver," someone breathed. "Clear silver. Oh God, her wolf must be beautiful."

Gordon helped her to sit up and then picked her up and put her on the couch. Before anyone could say anything, Alexis put her hand out for the female wolf that had cut her open.

"Come here, Stacy. Come on, no one will harm you here or I'll be doing some ass kicking myself." Phil looked over at the girl. "Can someone get the first aid kit? She's got a few cuts here."

Phil smiled. The girl had given as good as she'd gotten, it seemed. Dallas had a swollen eye and a busted lip, Austin was holding a napkin over his nose, and one of the pack was limping away. Phil nearly laughed out loud when CJ snickered loudly.

"Oh grow up, you oversized dog. She told you to leave her be, that she didn't want to come in here in the first place." CJ huffed at her mate and Phil laughed. He should have known she'd be on him fast. "Don't think I didn't notice that you were going to hit her yourself, you big mosquito. All of you go and find a place to sit or so help me, I'll find one for you."

Stacy refused treatment and stood near the door as the rest of them settled. She was skittish and afraid. He was sure everyone in the room could smell it. But she was also strong and very capable of taking them all on. She probably wouldn't win, but she'd hurt a few of them for their trouble.

"Phil, you have a book you wanted to share." He looked over at Nancy as she spoke. "The pretty book, didn't you want to share it with us? If you tell us about it maybe by then a few more furs will be less ruffled."

"Of course. Let me get it." He reached to the table, pulled it toward him, and bobbled it slightly. A small picture, a drawing really, slid out and he nearly fell over when he looked at it. It took him several seconds to realize that he'd lost the conversation.

"Phil, what is it? What have you found?" CJ took the picture from him when he handed it toward her. "Oh my God, it's her. It's Alexis."

And it was too, for the most part, except the hair was different. Alexis's was short and sassy while the woman in the picture had long and curly hair. The mouths were nearly the same, full and lush. But it was the eyes that made the two women the same, the same clear silvery shade that made him think of starless nights and bright summer days at the same time. CJ handed the picture to Alexis.

"My mother gave me this book. She said it's been in our family for generation after generation. The picture, while I've never seen it before, explains a lot. It tells me that you were meant to get this book." Phil handed the leather bound tome to her as he continued. "I've read this over...not in its entirety, but most of it. It's you. You're the shifter that it speaks of."

"I don't...what is that exactly? You make it sound as though I'm some sort of, well hell, I don't know, weird species." Alexis flushed. "I know there is something odd about me. I've known that I could heal and that I could turn into anything I want. I'd also been aware that I could heal myself, but only in very small things. But today, today was the first time I've been hurt so badly that—"

"You weren't breathing. She cut you badly and you stopped breathing. According to this book you're going to be the one who brings back the shifter." Phil looked over at Gordon before he spoke again. "And you, as her mate, are going to help her."

"Okay. For now, I'll believe you. But if you think I'm going to become some sort of breeding machine you can rethink that right fucking now. I'm not convinced about anything, but I'm willing to listen. What is a shifter and why are we...according to you, all gone?" Alexis sounded panicky and Gordon went to sit beside her.

"A shifter is just what it sounds like. They're a group of men or women who, at one time, could shift into any race and become one with them. It is said that when a shifter joined a mate, the mate could not tell and that every babe born to them would be as the counterpart. The only way for a shifter to be born of a pair was if they both were shifters."

"Are you saying that they bred themselves out? How ignorant is that?" Alexis handed him back the book while shaking her head. "I don't think so. I can't believe that anyone would be so stupid as to willingly become extinct. Were they so ashamed of what they were that they'd be willing to do that?"

Phil nodded and looked her right in the eye. "Yes."

~~~

Alexis stared at Phil without moving. Yes? They didn't want to be around so they'd done the unspeakable. She looked down at the book he'd given her again. The pictures there, ones of animals being slaughtered by men with pitchforks and sticks, were detailed and horrid. Some of the dead were half-human, shifting, she supposed, as they lay dying. She was horrified even more by what she saw, knowing that they had done this themselves.

There were several people standing around cages on another page. These animals were set in a large room with tables with the dead still bleeding upon them. She knew what this was. They were cutting into them, seeing what made them so different, trying to figure out what they were. She turned to the next page and saw the woman in the picture looking up at her.

She had a crown on, her body covered in silks. Her cape, long and dark, flowed down her body to the steps below. At her feet were others, people crying, their tears staining the guards' boots, puddling on the floor. Dead as well as the living huddled around her. She looked so...sad, Alexis thought. She looked at the words beneath the picture and suddenly knew what they meant. The language was as familiar to her as her own.

*I beseech thee to save us. I beg you to bring us home. Child of mine, you are our only hope.*

"She is speaking to me," Alexis said softly. "She is asking me to save them. Why? How does she think one person can bring an entire race back from what they've done?"

"No, she is begging you and your mate to do so. According to our legend, there is one who can do this and only one. The note from when you were found, it said that you'd be hunted and that the one who found you, loved you, would be richly rewarded. You have been. Both of you have," Phil said, his voice as low as hers had been. "Do you know what that reward is?"

She nodded. "Yes. I have Gordon." She looked over at Gordon and a thought occurred to her. "But Gordon is a werewolf. How am I supposed to bring them back if I'm the last? And what of this other man, the vampire? What does he have to do with all of this?"

"I don't know, love. You'll need to read this to know the answers to that. But I would imagine that there is a plan." He looked down at the drawing that she still held. "She had faith in you."

She nodded. It wasn't something she was going to fix overnight, but she knew with all her heart that she could do it. They could do it. She looked over at Gordon and kissed him on the mouth. He pulled her in for a much deeper one and then held her to him. She'd not realized just how much she'd needed that until then.

"I can release you from our bond. You've only to say that you accept. I don't know a lot of things yet, but I do know that I can release you from this bond." She held his face between her hands and looked him in the eyes. "Is this something you want?"

"No. I love you with all my heart and whatever we need to do, especially if it involves sex with you, I'm so there for you." He grinned before he kissed her again. "I do love you, Alexis, and whatever you need from me, I'm your mate for now and forever."

"He already knows. The vampire that is looking for you, he's been watching you for months." Alexis looked over at Stacy as she continued. "He knows where you are when you're in the house. He can't hear you, but he knows."

"And you know this how?" Austin asked the girl. "You've been helping him? Is that why you came here today? If it is, so help me I will make—"

"That's enough," Alexis snapped. "She hasn't been helping him. Don't you think one of you guys would have, I don't know, smelled her or something?" She turned to the girl. "Tell me why you stopped me. You ran in the road to stop me to talk. What is it? What do you know?"

Stacy looked around the room. Alexis wasn't sure if she would bolt or not but she seemed to calm for a moment. Alexis could see that she was terrified, but of what she still wasn't sure.

"One of the women in your house, they are with him." There was a sharp inhalation of breath, but Alexis didn't look away from Stacy. "I can't tell which one, but I know that it is someone close to you and the kids. She smells like you...not entirely, but like you." She looked over at Gordon and frowned. "I can't tell you what you want. I don't know. She has been meeting with the man, the old blood man, for years. His scent is strong on her. But it is on all of you. You are too close a pack for me to tell."

"I might be able to help." Alexis looked back at Phil as he spoke softly. "I might be able to tell who it is. I've been around all of you for months and I know your scents as well as anyone. But...."

When Phil didn't finish she knew she wasn't going to like it. And when Gordon stiffened beside her she knew he was going to be pissed about whatever he suggested. Then it occurred to her.

"Tell me, Phil. Tell me how we can tell who is selling me out to this man. And my family." She looked over at

Gordon as she continued. "Don't you want to know who our enemy is? I certainly do." She waited for him to explode, waited for Gordon to get all manly on her and tell her that she was stupid, but he nodded. Then he turned to Phil.

"What happens? How do you tell who is the bad guy in all this crap?" Phil glanced at Stacy then back at her before Gordon had a chance to continue. "Holy Christ, you have to bite her."

"Yes. With her blood I'll be able to sort through her mind and find everything she knows, all the things she has seen but never thought of as suspicious. She knows as well, but the information hasn't jelled into anything she can—"

"No," Jessie said quickly. "No, he wants your blood because he is a bloodsucking bastard and he'll kill you. Just like all his kind has done. You can't seriously think he wants anything from you but to drain you."

"I don't lie." Phil growled at her. "I have never seen the need to. But you, however, what is it you have to hide? Is there something you don't want us to know?" Phil stood up and moved toward her aunt. Alexis wanted to tell him to stop, to not think those things of her aunt, but she couldn't do it. When Aunt Jessie suddenly turned and left the room the slamming of the front door made her realize that Jessie had left the house. Alexis looked over at Gordon and the others. They were staring at her.

"And now?" she asked Gordon.

"Now we go forward. You knew that this might happen. That Jessie might be a part of what was going on." He looked around the room. "We all did."

Alexis nodded and turned to Phil again. She let him take her hand and pull it to his mouth. A low growl from Stacy startled her, but she didn't look at the girl. She was focused on the very sharp teeth that were coming to her wrist.

"I will deaden the pain with my saliva. Once that is done all you'll feel is a small pinch. Are you ready?" She nodded. "Then look at Gordon. He'll be happier that way."

She didn't just look at him, but kissed him. When she felt Phil's tongue slide against her wrist she was vaguely aware of a small pain, but nothing more. When Gordon pulled back, she moaned. There was something extremely needy in that kiss and she wanted to find a dark corner quickly and show him.

Phil had laid his head against the back of the couch. He looked drained, which was silly as he was usually the drainer. She flushed at her stupid joke and asked if he was all right.

"You're a shifter all right. A very powerful and full-blooded one, as a matter of fact," he said without moving. "Your blood, it's like a fine wine, an amazing drug, and a great night of sex all rolled into one." He grinned at her.

"I'm so glad you enjoyed it. Now tell me what this little experience told you about me other than I'm not anything different than you thought." She flushed when she noticed he had an erection. She knew that Gordon had one as well; he'd put her into his lap when she'd spoken to Phil. It took her several seconds to settle down, and when Gordon nipped at her shoulder, she nearly came.

"You're a full-blooded shifter, as I thought. And, as we've already ascertained, Jessie is in with the vampire. I don't suppose any of you know who he might be." He pulled the pillow over his lap as he continued. His wink at her made her face heat. They all looked toward Darcy as she entered the room.

"I know who he is. His name is Tom Garrison, and he came to the house the day my mother was killed. I heard Aunt Jessie telling him about the cameras...the one that is over the picture in that corner in the living room at home." She kept looking at Gordon as she spoke, something she'd never done until recently. She didn't point, but simply kept looking at Gordon. "He has one in the kitchen too, but I'm not sure where. But he watches us all the time."

"Yes. I remember him now. But I don't think I ever knew his name. After you were hurt I could only focus on you and helping you." Alexis looked over at Gordon when he cleared his throat. "You know something?"

"Paddy was changed by a Garrison. Probably the same guy. He more than likely knows what you are and wants you for his...dinner." She'd never thought of that and was nodding before he finished.

Stacy moved toward the door and she started to stop her, but the girl turned at the last minute and spoke to everyone in the room. "I have to go. But I'll keep watch." She glanced toward the door behind her before continuing. "Trust no one at your home. She might not be the only help he has."

She shifted quickly and was out the door before anyone could ask her what she meant. Alexis started to rise, but Gordon held her still. She turned to snap at him, but before she could say anything, he spoke in her ear.

"She's right. You need to figure out why he wants you and who else, if anyone, in the house is trying to help him. We think it's your Aunt Jessie, but who knows if your Aunt Glad is in on it too?" He pulled her closer still. "If she's in on it she'll know why he's hunting you and what he wants now that he's found you."

KATHI S. BARTON

# CHAPTER 17

Alexis had been quiet all the way back to her house. She'd said very little at the pack house, and when dinner was served she only picked at her food without eating. He wanted to tell her she needed to eat more, but a shake of CJ's head stopped him. Through their link as wolves she spoke to him.

*"She's had a lot thrown at her tonight. I'm guessing she's processing it, and if you try to make her do what you might think is right you're more than likely going to piss her off. It would me if you tried your he-man crap."* When he started to tell her that he was not going to be he-manlike she snorted at him. *"You know you were going to be, so just leave her alone and eat your stupid dinner. Men,"* she huffed at him.

He had wanted to be offended, but thought maybe she was right. Not that he'd tell her that, but he could think it. Gordon smiled now, wondering what she'd do to him if she knew that he was going to seduce Alexis out of her black mood.

"I don't want you to stay here tonight," she said as they pulled into her driveway. "I've had a really long day and I just want to go to bed. Alone. So I can talk to you tomorrow, all right?"

He didn't want to be pissed, he didn't want to be hurt either, but he was both. He took a couple of deep breaths before he spoke to her, and when he did he tried his best to sound like he was neither.

"No." *Well, that sucked*, he thought. "I don't want to go home. I want to be with you, Alexis. You're my mate and I need you."

"I've been...why?" Her sudden question startled him and before he could think about an answer, she was going on. "Is it because of the sex? I'm sure you've had much better and as for the mate stuff, I can't understand why you'd want to be mated to—"

He tore open the passenger side door as soon as she rolled to a stop. He was rounding the vehicle when she got out on her side. He wasn't sure what she was about to say because he pulled her into his body and kissed her, his mouth hard against hers and his body pressing her into the cold metal behind her.

Her hunger slammed into him. So hard, in fact, that he was sure she was going to take him rather than the other way around. When she moaned, wrapped her hand into his hair, and pulled him to her throat he opened his mouth over her rapidly beating pulse. Gordon felt his canines drop, saliva formed in his mouth, and all he could think about was marking her. Making her his for all time.

"I ache to take you. Now, right now." Gordon rocked into her hard and heard her moan again. "Christ, you'll never make it inside."

He let his wolf go just a bit. His claws formed and he tore her pants from her. Her scent hit his senses immediately and he growled deep. Licking a path down her neck to her throat again, he tore at his own pants and freed his cock. The cool air of the evening did nothing to slow him. Lifting her up by her ass, he slammed into her as he sank his teeth into her neck.

Her scream filled the air. He couldn't stop now if his very life depended on it. Fucking her hard and holding her still with his teeth, he felt his balls tighten up, his climax beating at him as hard as he was at her. When she lifted his wrist to her mouth he knew she was going to bite him and he wanted it. Wanted her to take from him as much as he was from her. When her teeth broke the skin and she suckled he came with a roar. His seed spewed from him and into her so hard that he was lightheaded from it. But he wasn't finished, wasn't nearly satisfied. When he lifted his head he knew what she was seeing. His beast was there in his eyes, his canines were long.

"Turn around," was all he could manage. When she didn't move fast enough he pulled from her still pulsing body and shoved her against the trunk of the car. Before she could protest, if that was even in her mind, he was deep inside of her again, her pussy sucking him in and soaking him.

"Fuck me. Oh please, Gordon, fuck me." He couldn't think beyond her pussy, and her words only took him closer to the edge. Reaching around her, he slid his fingers into her slit. She was wet, soaking wet, and hot. When he pinched her clit, her sheath rippled along his cock. When he did it again she put her hand over his and rocked back.

"Come, Alexis. Come now and I'll make you mine." He licked her shoulder again. "I want to claim you in the way of our kind. Come with me, baby, and you'll be mine."

She came quickly. Her body stiffened beneath his and he bit as she screamed again. This bite was deeper, harder than ever before. It would also leave a mark, a mark of his teeth into her flesh that all would see. He jerked his mouth hard, tearing at her tender skin, and let his climax roll again. Gordon felt the connection between them snap into place, much like a rubber band against his wrist.

They had truly mated and bonded.

He didn't move. He actually wasn't sure if he'd be able to after that. Alexis was resting her head against the car and her body was limp. He moved her hair from her face and saw that her eyes were closed, but she seemed all right. After watching her for a few more seconds he realized she was asleep or unconscious.

He pulled from her gently, but even that had him wanting her again. He wanted to wake her and take her again, but thought if he did they'd both be sleeping where they were. He didn't think he'd have anything left to walk, much less carry her into the house afterwards. Smiling, he adjusted his clothing and then wrapped her in what was left of his shirt and took her into his arms. He was nearly to the house when he heard the first baying of the wolf.

Stilling, he tried to pinpoint where the wolf was. He had a pretty good idea it was Stacy, but not completely. Once inside the house he lifted Alexis higher into his arms and set the alarms, glad now that she'd given him the codes. When he turned around he nearly dropped his mate when he saw someone walking along the hallway toward the kitchen.

Setting Alexis on her feet, Gordon put his hand over her mouth and woke her. She smiled up at him before she looked worried. He knew just how she felt. When he leaned in to whisper in her ear another person walked along the hallway toward the kitchen. Alexis stiffened in his arms, but made no sound.

"It's Aunt Jessie. Where is she going in the middle of the night?" They both heard the door open then close and Alexis turned to look up at him.

"She's not alone. Someone else went that way just ahead of her. Go carefully and when I tell you to move, do it." She nodded. He wasn't sure she'd do it, but at least if he had to shove her out of the way she wouldn't be able to blame him. He heard a voice before they got to the doorway.

"Can't tell you anything if I don't know the answer, now can I?" The pause made him think she was on the phone as he didn't hear any other person. "No. No, that won't be necessary. He hasn't come by yet. When he does I know how to get rid of him. I just don't know why you can't just…what do you mean you can't kill the prick? I told you before if you want her you're going to have to cut me some slack here."

Alexis turned to look at him. Her face was full of shock. As the conversation grew more heated, another voice spoke up. This one startled him so badly that he couldn't move. And they nearly got caught when the door opened from the kitchen and two people walked out.

"I don't know why we didn't get rid of that wolf when he first showed up. This is stuff that should have been cleared up way before all this went down." Wilbur, the delivery man, was there too. "You'd think we'd be better at this by now, what with all the killings we been doing for Tom. Where is that man anyway?"

"He said he'd meet me tomorrow at his house," Jessie said as she headed for the stairs with Wilbur in tow. "I'm thinking he might be wanting us to go with him when he leaves here. Whatcha think?"

"I'm thinking Glad might be right and you are the dumbest woman alive. Why on earth would you be meeting a cold blooded killer on his own turf?"

Their voices faded as they climbed the stairs. When the door to a room closed Alexis turned to him and stared up into his face. She was quiet, but he could see a world of emotions swirling in her eyes.

"I'm not leaving here. I know that's what you're thinking, so you can stop that right now." He brushed away a tear before he continued. "We won't let them win, Alexis. And besides, we're mated now. Nothing can hurt us."

"They'll hurt us in other ways," she said as she laid her head on his chest. "They both...." She looked up at him. "Why?"

He pushed her head back to this chest. He didn't know. Most people did things for greed. But this woman seemed to be doing it for simple pleasure. Gordon didn't know yet, but he'd find out.

Picking her up, he took her to their bedroom. She didn't say anything about him leaving again and he didn't press when she insisted on looking at the book that Phil had given her. He wanted to tell her that in the morning things would look better, but he could feel her hurt at what was going on. When she pulled open the wall that he'd thought was a computer area he could only stare at what she revealed to him.

The wall unit was huge when it was closed, but when open it was massive. The doors only hid the room beyond them and the equipment she housed there. When she sat at the large desk, he walked in and sat in one of the many chairs that faced it. She was booting up the computer when she started to explain.

"I'm not what…my family thought I was a chemical engineer." He watched as the screens behind her lit up. "I've been employed by the best of the best. I'm still employed by our government. I find things. Mostly people, but I sometimes get called out to find treasures, bombs, and even an occasional murderer."

He watched the screen directly behind her start to focus on something. It took him several seconds to figure out she was looking at her house. When the screen moved he watched as it seemed to be stopping and starting again, searching for…well, he wasn't sure what it was searching for.

"Are you looking for someone? Or something?" She grinned at him and he looked back at the screen. "The phone call. You're tracking the phone call, aren't you?"

"Yes. I have this enhanced signal booster that can back trace a call. The call was made from this house and all I need to do now is find the source. I'm thinking I might know who the person is, but…well, I don't know where he lives."

"Tom. You're looking for Tom. Is he the one that you think is talking to your aunt and Wilbur?" She nodded at first then shook her head, seemingly undecided. "You think he might be looking for you *and* someone else then? Who? Do you know?"

"Sort of. I know that Tom changed Paddy, or at least the vampire part. And, for whatever reason, he wants Darcy. I figure he's going to use her against me. Maybe that wasn't his plan at first, but I think that might be where this is headed now. I got the feeling he was going to keep her for something, but I didn't know what."

They both watched as the screen kept zigzagging across. He was dizzy watching it and looked back down at her. She was looking at the screen in front of her with a frown. He started to ask her what was wrong when the screen froze. She looked up at him.

He didn't like the look. Slowly, he looked back up at the large screen behind her and tried to make out where it was. When he figured it out, it was all he could do not to howl. Christ, the man was living on pack land. And not only that, he was living in CJ's old house.

~~~

Paddy paced the yard. He'd been waiting on Tom for over an hour. He had a plan he wanted to share with him and hadn't gone to the house like he should have. Plus, he had to pee. If the prick didn't show up soon he was headed for the woods. After another twenty minutes Paddy went to the edge of the property and into the deeper woods to take care of business. While he was just pulling out his cock to urinate a car pulled up. Paddy nearly peed on his own shoe when he saw who got out.

He wasn't really surprised to see Tom being handed out. The guy couldn't take a shit without fifty people there to hand him a sheet of toilet paper to wipe with. Eating dinner was something that Paddy had only joined him for once, and thought he'd die before going back to sit through "courses." And all the plates and silverware completely confused him. Nah, he thought, give him a brown paper bag, burger and fries, and a beer and he had all the courses he wanted.

The next person out of the car was Jessie. He'd never liked her and seeing her hanging all over Tom like she was his...Paddy frowned. They were lovers, he just realized. And he realized something else. She was Tom's source, too. Watching the two of them touch each other and acting like—*gross,* he thought—randy goats, he nearly turned away. But he heard Tom speak and he froze in his tracks.

"Did the moron show up?" Jessie shook her head. "I give you one job and this is how you do it? Jessie, I've told you before, when I give you something to do I expect it to be done promptly. Not when you get around to it. I'll not have anyone thinking they can get away with not following the simplest of directions."

"I have a plan. I'm going to make sure his scent is all over my niece. He left some of his clothes behind when he departed the house the last time and I've put them in with some of Alexis's clothes in a trash bag. Every time I go by it I give it a good shake so that his scent is all over hers."

Jessie slid her hand over Tom's chest and Paddy backed up, suddenly unsure of this situation.

He stepped on a log as he moved and it snapped. The sound was loud in the otherwise noisy forest. Everything around him grew quiet in an instant. The couple and the driver looked toward where he was standing. Paddy knew that any moment he was going to die.

The driver took out his gun and started to where Paddy was hiding. He didn't have time to move, so he stood perfectly still. The closer they got to where he was hiding, the more terrified he became. The way they were standing, with Tom just behind the driver and Jessie with her back to the men and her gun out too, there was no way they'd miss him if they saw him. He never took his eyes from them even though the need to flee was strong.

Just before they took a step into the woods, a large male deer leapt out of the tree line beside them and had them all turn as one toward the giant stag. The roar of gunfire was terrifying. Paddy watched as the stag fell first to his knees then to the ground. He was dead long before his head fell to the side. With eyes wide open, blood spilled to the earth and he took his last breath. Paddy had never been so happy to see something else die in his entire life.

"That was fucking awesome," the driver said as the last echo faded away. Paddy had fallen to his ass at some point and didn't even bother looking up to see what he was talking about. "Did you see that sucker bleed out? Christ, let's scare up—"

"Shut up and get that piece of shit out of here." Tom slapped the driver hard in the face and knocked him down. "And this one too."

The gun was still out and pointed at Jessie's head so quickly that Paddy nearly screamed for her to run. The bullet went in her forehead and out the back of her head, and Paddy knew she was able to watch her own body drop. Tom had just killed his source, and he had a sudden feeling that he was next.

Paddy felt his urine run down his leg as he thought of what lay in wait for him the next time he crossed paths with Tom. When the driver picked up the dead woman, tossed her on top of the deer carcass, and began to drag the two bodies away, Paddy made the decision to get as far away as he could. Right now, right fucking now.

As soon as Tom went into the house and he was sure that the driver was well away, Paddy gathered up as many leaves and pinecones as he could find and tossed them over where he'd been, hoping to mask his scent. After waiting another hour, and after the driver returned and went inside, Paddy left. He was nearly to his car when his cell phone went off. Knowing it was Tom he broke the phone in half, tossed both pieces into the road, and drove over them when he started up his car.

Next stop, he thought, was out of there.

# CHAPTER 18

Austin looked down at the lease that lay on his desk. He'd not asked any questions when he'd okayed the renting of the little house, but now he wondered if he should have. He looked up when Phil started talking again.

"It was done completely by a third party. The person who needed it was told that it would be on a month to month basis until the owner could figure out whether or not to sell." Phil got up to pace, something he only did when he was nervous or pissed. Austin figured it was a good deal of both.

"How long has the man been renting the house? And when did he move in?" Austin looked over at his mate. She was looking very pregnant and he was concerned about the added stress. "If it's month to month, I say we just kick his ass out then kill his sorry ass."

"You might be ri—"

"No." Dallas cut Phil off. "You might want to rethink that. At least when he's right there at our doorstep we can keep an eye on him." Dallas looked at him. "It's your call, of course, but I would have my friends close and my enemies closer."

Austin agreed. But it wasn't just his decision to make. He looked over at his brother and his mate. Alexis had the most to lose in this, and also the most to gain. Gordon would do whatever he asked of him, but Alexis…well, he wasn't sure what she'd do. He looked over at CJ. "The house is still in your name. Ultimately, it's my decision, but I would very much like to hear what you have to say." He winced when she glared at him. "I mean, I would consider anything you have to say and weigh it against what is good for us all."

"Good save, doggy boy, but not good enough." CJ got up, walked to where Alexis and Gordon were sitting, and knelt before them. "The house is secure, both this one and yours. We had cameras set up all over the house, and if he didn't disable them then we can see him as well as, if not better than, if he was sitting here in the house with us. He won't get into either house unless he has a tank, and I'm pretty sure that we would all hear that sucker coming a mile or two away. So my question is, what do you want to do?"

Austin knew she was right. This directly involved them more than it did pack. But still, the man was—

*"Oh hush up. I can hear your thoughts, you know."* He mentally stuck his tongue out at CJ. *"Yeah, you do that now, but I'm betting you can think of better uses for that tongue than sticking it out there uselessly."*

Austin felt his body harden for her. She knew what she was doing to him and it took him several seconds to realize that he'd missed something. When he tried to concentrate on the conversation CJ sent him a mental picture of what he'd done to her last night.

*"Behave or I'll spank your ass again. What are you doing now? You know that Phil thinks they're both safe here. If they want to go up against this bastard they could very well be the only ones to walk away unscathed."*

*"Or not."* He felt her fear then. *"What if he's wrong? I can't...I won't lose either of them. Not now. We have to protect them as our own."*

Austin had never been prouder of anyone than he was at that moment. He sent her his love through their connection and felt it returned to him. Then he settled in to listen to the plan. And in the end he thought it a very good one.

They were to confront him. They all agreed that it was the best bet in bringing out the man who was in charge. Phil said there had to be a higher power in all this, and he was going to check with his father and mother to see what they knew. His dad was a vampire and had just as much power as his mate. He thought that the two of them could come up with an answer. Then there was the changing of Paddy to vampire. How would Tom have gotten permission to change Paddy? There had to be someone else, someone that would have enough power in the vampire council to give him what he needed to get what he wanted.

"When you go to the house, what are you going to say? 'Hello, I'm here to kick your ass and bend over so I can do it?'" Dallas grinned as he spoke. "I'm pretty sure all that's going to do is piss him off more. I was thinking maybe you could simply ask him if he has a cup of sugar."

"Nah," Phil chimed in. "That won't work. He's full-blooded. He won't have that in his kitchen."

Hilarity broke out. They were all tired and seemingly not taking things as seriously as they should have been. Austin was about to call it quits for the night. After twenty some hours of going over different strategies, he figured they all needed a good night's sleep, but Glad came in the room.

"Has anyone seen Jessie? She said she had a date and hasn't returned." Austin could feel her worry and fear. "She normally calls when she's spending the night somewhere else. And before you ask, yes, I called the delivery man. He's not seen her either."

It was on the tip of his tongue to ask her if Jessie was meeting Tom, but a sharp look from Phil warned him to stay quiet. Instead, Phil went to her and put his arm around her. He began to rub her bare skin and suddenly, Austin knew what he was doing. He was trying to get a place to draw blood.

"Oh my, Glad, what have you done here?" She tried to turn to see what Phil meant when she inhaled sharply. "See, you have a cut here. Let me put something over it. It looks a little red."

Austin just bet it did. He was smiling when he realized CJ was staring at him. He was about to share what was going on when Phil suddenly put his finger into his mouth. He looked over at both him and CJ and winked. Austin wasn't sure, but he'd bet his last dollar that not only could Phil track Gladys, but he was reasonably sure he could find her entire lineage.

When they disappeared down the hall Alexis cleared her throat. "He could have simply asked her, you know?"

Austin tried to keep his laughter to a low rumble, but when Gladys and Phil returned with a large Band-Aid on her shoulder, her words confirmed that she had no idea what had just happened.

"I don't know how I could have cut myself. Why just this morning I was…you don't suppose one of those kids accidentally threw something at me, do you?" Phil shook his head, mirth all over his face. "That poor boy. We won't mention it. He'll feel bad for me."

Austin could only hope that at some point he could breathe again. When she finally left the room he was laughing so hard and trying not to show it he was sure he broke something. He was almost afraid to look at Phil again.

~~~

Alexis paced her room. She thought about leaving it several times, but every time she started for the door she would stop just short of opening it. She turned to look at Gordon when he laughed.

"I don't think you're going to solve much by wearing a hole in the carpet. Come here." She glared at him and continued pacing. "Alexis, come here and let's work this out."

"Why?" She had an idea what he wanted and how he wanted to "work things out," but she just wasn't in the mood. At least she didn't think she was. "Sex does not solve everything, contrary to popular belief."

"No," he said, smiling. "It won't solve anything, but it will certainly relax you enough to think things through afterwards."

Alexis stood very still when he stood. She watched as he started to unbutton his shirt and pull it from his pants, and she licked her suddenly dry lips.

"You would have been safer if you had simply left when you could. Maybe there's a way to reverse this thing." She pulled at her blouse, the heat in the room suddenly a little too much. "I bet Phil's mom knows somebody."

"I don't want anyone to reverse this. I want you." The shirt landed on the floor next to her towel she'd discarded earlier. "Come here, Alexis. I want to make love to you."

He moved like the wolf he was. She could smell him too, earthy and warm. She knew that if he were to go into the woods right now no one would be able to find him by scent.

She looked out the window and watched his reflection as he came up behind her. When he cupped her breasts and pulled her back against his chest, she moaned. His cock nudged her ass and she felt her pussy cream.

"Run with me. Let's go outside and run for a while. Then, if you're really good, I'll lay you on a carpet of spring flowers and take you to heights you've never been before." She turned her head to look at him as he spoke. "I can and you know it. Come on. Then we'll come back here and sleep the day away."

It was tempting. Very tempting, as a matter of fact. She felt something stir inside of her and startled when Gordon growled at her.

"Your wolf is stirring. She wants mine." Gordon lowered his hands to her hips and held her still while he rocked into her ass again, his cock hard as stone. "I want you as well. Come outside with me and play, Alexis. Shift into your wolf and let's run through the fields again."

The last time she'd been a wolf they'd had sex several times in the open field. It had been fantastic. Then they'd made love as humans several more times until neither of them could move, and had taken a nap out of doors to regain their strength to walk back to the house. She pulled from his arms and moved to the door to the passage as his cell phone rang.

"It's Dallas. I have to take—"

"Don't," she begged him. "Please, not yet. Text him. Tell him...tell him whatever it is that...tell him that we need one hour. Just one hour."

Gordon looked undecided and she let her wolf stir again. Once she'd figured out what it felt like it was easy. His moan/growl had her wet and needy and he knew it.

"You're going to pay for this," Gordon told her as he started doing as she asked. "Once we get outside you're so going to pay for this."

She didn't wait for him, but ran for the door laughing. She was stripping off her clothes and shifting before he nearly caught up with her. By the time she was flying out of the waterfalls she could hear him cussing at her to wait. She was soaring to the sky again when she felt the danger. By then it was too late.

# CHAPTER 19

The pack of wolves was just below her. She could see that Gordon was just coming out of the lake when he saw them too. He looked up to where she had landed, but kept low too. She didn't know why they looked so different from Gordon until he spoke to her.

*"They're wild. We're bigger and stronger and, because we can think like a human even as a wolf, we tend to fight better too."* He moved as he spoke to her, but still remained hidden. *"Stay where you are and I'll see if I can draw them away from you. Then I want you to—"*

*"No fucking way. I'm way up here and you're down there at their level. I'll be the one to draw them away from you. I can go into places that you—"*

*"Alexis,"* he growled at her. *"If you so much as move from that branch I will beat your ass for you. I'll not have you endangering your life for me. Now, I want you to stay up there. I've contacted Austin and Dallas and they are coming here now."*

She growled back at him. It was either that or shift, beat the wolves, and then him. She was sure that she'd hurt herself badly if she tried shifting to a wolf from that height, but might have been willing to chance it except for the man who came into the clearing behind another dozen or so wolves.

Tom was walking along a seemingly narrow path. Alexis couldn't really make out how wide it was as she'd never seen it from that vantage point before. All she could see was that it led to the lake and even down along it for a ways. As she was telling Gordon, she saw Paddy going from tree to tree behind the pack and Tom.

It occurred to her that he was stalking Tom, not with him as she first thought. As she watched him move she also came to the conclusion that he was really terrible at sneaking. She wondered why he didn't simply shift into his wolf, which had to be much quieter than his human was.

*"If he does, then he'll be naked when the time comes to fight."* She startled at the voice that sounded right next to her. *"You should know that taking your blood was sort of an open highway for us to speak."*

Alexis thought about Phil and then she cut off his dick with a sharp rock. She knew the moment he got the message because she could feel his pained thoughts. Grinning to herself, she sobered when she saw that Darcy was being dragged toward the group with the pack. That terrified her to the point she nearly shifted and attacked.

*"Don't. If you go in now, all will be lost. Think, love. What is it you think you can do and not get anyone killed?"* She wanted to snarl at Gordon, but before she could Phil started again.

*"If you go in half-cocked, then...well, my own will be much safer. However, if you get killed in the process, your mate will suffer as well."*

*"You do know that at this moment I hate you both very much."* But she did stop to think.

Tom was below her now, but there were also several dozen wolves, all of which had very sharp teeth and could cut her to ribbons. Behind them was Paddy, but he seemed to be doing nothing to help. She didn't think he was with the vampire below her, but she just couldn't be sure about that. Then there was her niece. Darcy was as innocent as they all were evil. Suddenly the girl looked up at her and smiled.

*"You can hear me?"* It was really too much to hope that she could, but she'd never tried to communicate with the child this way before. Darcy dropped her head and Alexis nearly cried out in frustration.

*"Yes. You sound funny, but I can hear you. I can hear...it sounds like Mr. Gordon too, but I'm not sure."* Alexis moved a branch lower as Darcy continued. *"He wants to change me. He wants me to be his day walker. I don't want to do that, Aunt Alexis. Please help me."*

*"I am, baby."* She looked over at Gordon, who was crouched low behind a fallen log. She wondered why they hadn't seen him yet and remembered her vantage point. *"Gordon is coming toward you from the tree just to your left. Can you see him at all?"*

Darcy raised her head only to have her face slapped. Alexis let out a sharp cry and flew off so that she wouldn't be tempted to go down and rip Tom's eyes out. She wanted the man dead in the worst way.

*"I can't see him. And don't worry about this man hitting me. When you save me, I'm going to kick his bottom."* Alexis came back, landed just above the group in another tree, and sent her niece all the love she could.

*"Darcy, love, can you pretend to faint? I can come a bit closer to you if you distract them for me."*

Alexis wanted to tell Gordon no, but before she could Darcy did just as he'd asked her to. Gordon moved up another ten feet or so and was nearly to them when the group seemed to turn to the left as one.

Alexis could see the larger wolves coming at them at a full out run. She was both terrified and awed by the beauty at the same time. She knew that the larger wolf at the head of the pack was Austin and could see why he was alpha.

*"I'm much prettier than him,"* Gordon told her. *"You should know that. And when this nonsense is over, I'm going to show you just how much bigger I can get when you're naked beneath me."*

Her entire body reacted to his words. And she nearly moaned before a movement caught her eye. Paddy was moving up behind Tom with a knife in his hands. She knew the exact moment when the vampire knew he was there. She watched in horror as Paddy put his knife down and spoke to Tom.

"I've come to make a bargain with you. I don't want you to kill me like you did Jessie. What will it take to keep myself alive?" Paddy nodded toward his daughter. "Her?"

Tom laughed. "I've already got her, you moron. What the hell else could you possibly offer me? And as soon as that cunt of a shifter shows up I'll have her as well. You,"

Tom said as he pulled out a gun, "have outlived your usefulness to me and my cause."

The sharply barked "no" was all that Paddy was able to say before the gun went off. A second shot, this one not nearly as loud, sounded at almost the same time. When Tom dropped to one knee Alexis thought he had fallen, but it seemed someone had shot the man. Paddy fell forward as a gun slipped from his fingers.

Alexis could only stare as Tom pulled his long sword free and took Paddy's head from his shoulders. A scream from Darcy brought Alexis from the nightmare.

The wolves coming to help were too far away when Tom suddenly turned toward Darcy. He had his hand raised with his sword coming toward her. Alexis knew that if Darcy was going to be saved it had to be now and it had to be her. Dropping to the ground, she shifted and landed at nearly the same time.

~~~

Gordon nearly shifted to go after her when he saw her dropping. He knew that for the rest of his days, whenever he thought of her falling to the ground, he'd still have shivers of terror run through him. But when she stood behind the vampire and swiped at him, Gordon knew that she would conquer.

"What have we here? Another wolf?" Gordon moved closer as Tom spoke. "You know that I have a fine collection of beautiful pelts at home, and your silver one will fill it out nicely."

Alexis growled low and deep, masking any sound the pack made running faster now toward them. Gordon reached out to his brother and alpha.

*"If you don't get here in the next several seconds I'm going to have to move in without you. He has my mate and I'm afraid he's going to kill her."* Gordon moved closer still. He wasn't afraid of the pack, but he was afraid for the safety of his mate. If he made the wrong move they'd kill her because of their vast number.

*"I'm coming. Did you have to do this all the way across our land and the other side of hers? Christ, we're moving as fast as we've ever moved."* Gordon snarled at his brother's comment. *"Calm down, Gordon. You'll do none of us any good if you get either of you killed. I'm coming. We're all coming."*

The pack hit the wolves with the vampire as one. Nearly fifty fully grown and not so grown wolves had more than half of the wild wolves killed before they could get away. In a matter of seconds the ground was covered in blood.

Gordon leapt up and was after Tom when the man turned with Alexis as her wolf suddenly in front of him, his huge hands wrapped around her throat. Gordon stopped so suddenly that dirt flew up at Tom and sprinkled his face and hair.

Gordon couldn't shift fast enough. He was standing before the two of them. He looked at his mate then at the man who held her.

"You harm her and I will hunt you down, stake you to the ground, and roast marshmallows over your burning body when the sun comes up." He took a step forward when Alexis whimpered. "Let her go and let's take care of this man to man."

Tom laughed and spittle ran down his chin as he licked Alexis's furred cheek. "You think to threaten me then you want me to do something for you? You're very stupid if you think your puny little wolf is going to scare me. I know what a wolf of her caliber is worth. What do you think I wanted the brat for? I turned the father as a lark. Having his daughter to breed will make me rich."

The movement beside him didn't make him turn. He'd know his brother's scent anywhere. Smiling, he looked Tom up and down then to his face again. He was terrified if he let himself think about where Alexis was and how this man could hurt her, so he tried not to look directly at her.

"Turning a human without permission is a crime punishable by death. You don't really think that the alpha around here is going to let you do that, do you? I mean, first off, she's merely a child; secondly…well secondly, I'm going to kill you so all your plans are for naught."

At least he hoped so. Gordon took a step forward and Austin moved with him. His wolf was so large that he reached nearly to Gordon's hip at the back. Alexis whimpered again and he looked at her. When their eyes connected she looked to his left then back at him. She did this twice more before he felt the other vampire.

"Hello, Tom. It's been a very long time." Gordon glanced at the newcomer and didn't have the slightest idea if the man was friend or foe. When he spoke again Gordon felt his world tilt. "I've come to claim my rights as your maker."

"Maker," Gordon said about the same time he saw Phil come into view. "I don't think you have any rights, maker or not. He has my mate and things are going to get nasty really fastlike if he doesn't let her go."

The man put his hand on Gordon's shoulder and he felt the immediate connection. There was something very…warm he supposed, about the man's touch, almost as if they'd known each other for a very long time.

"Gordon, please let my father have his say. This will go a good deal quicker if you do." Phil stood on his left as the stranger kept where he was on his right. "I called my father when I heard the name. It took him some time, but he remembered his child after some help from my mom."

"She most certainly did not help. If truth be told, she was more of a hindrance than help." Mr. Campbell paused a few seconds before he continued. "And if you tell her I said that, I will deny it with my last breath."

"It well may be your last breath, you old turd. What is the meaning of this?" Mrs. Campbell, Gordon thought, looked over at the man who still held Alexis. "Tom, you'd best listen or Rod here will be forced to take serious action. And just so you know, the council is very interested in the murder of a local human."

"I did no such thing. And I think you are all missing the point here. I have this she-bitch and I'm not letting her go until I get what I need." Tom looked down at Alexis before he looked back at them. "You come any closer and my death will be nothing compared to this bitch."

It only took a second, a mere blink for things to go from bad to over. The silver wolf in Tom's hands was suddenly gone; fur tangled in his fingers, but the wolf herself was nowhere to be seen. The screech of the hawk high above them had each of them turning skyward.

Gordon had a second, no more, to realize that she was the most beautiful creature he'd ever seen before she was soaring toward him, her wings wide. When she narrowly missed him as she landed on the ground just inches from him, he watched as she hopped from one foot to the other before settling. She didn't take her eyes from Tom.

"She's a shifter," Phil's father said softly, almost reverently. "Phil said that she was, but to see her...holy Christ, no wonder he wants her so badly."

Tom turned and, as he started forward again, the cane he always carried seemed to morph into a long sword. As it moved toward Gordon, the air seemingly slicing open, he didn't have a second to ponder his own death and the loss of his life with Alexis. But the blade didn't touch him...nothing did. The sound around the forest stilled. And before him lay Tom Garrison, his throat sliced from ear to ear.

# CHAPTER 20

Alexis poured the last of the soap into the forms. She watched the hot liquid fill each section of the metal and smiled when she thought of the people who would be using this very soap by the end of the week. She glanced to her left when she heard Gordon cussing again.

"This is shit. Every time I follow your directions all I get is shit. What am I doing wrong?" He didn't look to her like he was helping so much as he was trying on what she sold. He was covered from head to toe in white powder and bits of herbs he'd tried to cut up for her earlier. Before she could set down her pot, Darcy came to his rescue. Again.

"Look, Uncle Gordon, I showed you before. If you don't let it get to temperature then it won't get hard. And if it doesn't get hard, nobody will buy it from Aunt Alexis. Then where will we be but out on the streets selling this poop to anybody who will give us a penny for it?" Alexis thought she heard her say, "If somebody would give us a penny for it," but wasn't sure.

"You, young lady, have been hanging out with my sister-in-law too much. Just keep the snide comments to yourself and show me what I did wrong." He grinned at her before he kissed her forehead. "There's a good girl. And if you finish this batch for me I'll give you fifty bucks toward your car."

Alexis simply rolled her eyes. At the rate Darcy was going she'd have a better car than she did and for very little out of pocket cash on her end. Gordon had agreed to help in the barn three times a week, but mostly he hired one of the kids to do his part while he watched. When Alexis was finished with her pouring she looked over at him and he winked.

"You do know you'll never get the hang of this if you keep paying someone else to do it for you, right?" She shook her head when he grinned bigger. "I see. So just how rich are you making my nieces and nephews with this 'help' you're giving me?"

"You'll never know. They've been sworn to secrecy." He moved toward her, slow and easy like the big wolf that he was. "Darcy, will you watch things in here for a few minutes? I want to talk to your aunt outside."

"I can't go outside with you until I get this batch finished. Then I have to go to the pack house and help with the decorations for CJ's baby shower. She said I had to be there on time or she was going to hunt me down." Alexis had discovered that she and CJ had a great deal in common, but CJ was much scarier about things when they didn't go as she'd planned. "Then there is your mom."

That stopped him in his tracks and had him frowning. "What about my mom? She's not coming over, is she? Please tell me that you didn't tell on me again."

Alexis started to laugh and tell him his mother knew everything, but she didn't. She thought she'd keep that to herself. She moved to get another batch off the stove when he rushed to take it from her. He poured while she tamped things down.

They worked side by side for several minutes without speaking. They quickly poured the liquid soap into the newly purchased molds and added the seal to the ones that had hardened enough that she could press it into. She hoped that he hadn't noticed the ones in the basket near the door when he came in, but it was too much to hope that the ex cop wouldn't see them.

"The wolves, did you order those before or after the pack accepted you?" She looked at him and quickly away. "Alexis?"

"Before. But I'd met you already." She picked up the next mold and put it onto the cooling rack with the others. Darcy went out the door with a small wave. "I thought I could convince your mother and sisters to buy more if I had them in stock."

He nodded as he reached into the basket and pulled one out. "They're very beautiful. And I'm sure that whoever carved them knew that you weren't using them as simple nature art either."

He handed her the bar and she looked at it. When he took it back and showed her the small human footprints that the wolf left behind in the soap, she looked up at him, startled.

"I didn't see that. I swear I didn't order…do you know who did these for me?" He nodded. "Is it someone we know?" Again, he nodded.

She tried to think who she had met that carved. The soap molds that she bought were all one of a kind. The person who did hers did custom work, and when she'd placed her order for the wolves, he'd laughed and told her it would be his pleasure. The molds had also been shipped several weeks earlier than she'd been told they would. She looked down at the tiny signature that was in the lower left hand corner. CWF and the year was all it said.

"It's Connor, isn't it?" She looked up at him as she asked, suddenly sure that was who it was.

"He wasn't very graceful as a kid. He was forever tripping over his own feet and had a broken ankle at least twice a summer for a few years running. Our dad showed him how to carve using a knife and a few simple tools. Mom was terrified that he was going to cut his fingers off or slice open an artery and die before he could grow into his feet. He got really good at it." He picked up the mold that she'd emptied that morning. "He loved to carve in relief and made a pretty good name for himself by the time he was sixteen. When he turned eighteen and needed money for school, he started carving enough and selling his stuff online. By the time he was in his twenties, he was a millionaire."

Alexis looked at the bar of soap in a whole new light. Connor had seen them when he'd been in there the previous week. "He never said anything. He just sort of nodded in their general direction when I asked if he'd seen them and he said, 'yeah,' like it was no big deal."

"It's not to him. He doesn't make them for a living. He simply likes doing it because it makes him happy."

Gordon moved closer to her as she backed up. "Where do you think you're going, love?"

When he talked to her in that "I'm going to fuck you until you can't walk again soon" voice, she felt herself respond. She moved back more out of overwhelming need than anything else. He moved with her and when she put her hand up to stop him, he took it to his mouth and kissed it softly.

"I wasn't sure how you'd feel about me since I…since I killed Tom." The first night they'd been together, he'd simply held her. Then since, he'd not stayed at her house. "I didn't know what to think about everything."

"The Council of Weres had to talk to me. Well, me and Austin. I told them that I didn't want to leave and form my own pack just yet. Austin had to let them know that he was all right with me staying on for a little while and letting me keep my pack."

She knew that. Nancy, Gordon's mother, had told her that it was a big deal to have the council decide in your favor about things like this. Wolves, especially alphas like Gordon and his brother, could easily come to want to kill each other over territorial rights. Gordon had had to sign in blood, his own, that he had no desire to take his brother's pack, and didn't want to do anything but serve and protect his brother's claim. That had taken just over two weeks…until just after her own trial of sorts had ended.

"Are they still sticking to their decision that I killed that man in self defense?" She shuddered when she thought of what she'd done. "Are they going to change their mind and come after me?"

She'd been her bird when it started. Terror had gripped her when she saw the cane moving toward Gordon. She didn't know a lot about wolves, or vampires for that matter, but knew that silver was something that could and would kill them. She'd seen that same knife when Tom had come to her sister's house and knew that he would kill whomever it struck. She also knew that he planned to kill Gordon, and she refused to lose another person in her life.

"When I saw the knife coming toward me I thought...." She looked up at him, scared of what he meant. "You'd be alone and I'd never get to see you large with our babe. Lots of other thoughts came to mind, but that one hurt me the most."

"I couldn't let him kill you. He would have, you know. And me shifting to the wolf was the only thing I could do. She wanted him dead and I let her go."

The wolf, her wolf, had snarled at her when she'd landed at Gordon's feet as a bird and not a wolf. She'd tried to calm her, speak to her as if she was another being when she saw the cane change. The wolf inside of her seemed to say "mine," and Alexis let her have it. It wasn't until her claw, the one that was suddenly at her wrist even as the feathers on her arms were still fading away, was at Tom's neck that Alexis realized that the shift hadn't hurt at all, and neither did killing a man.

"You saved my life and those of the others around us...especially Rod and Hope Campbell and my brother." He moved closer and she backed up again, this time into the table behind her. "Are you still concerned that they will sentence you? They won't. Rod said that you were well within your rights as my mate to kill the man."

She'd heard him say that too. He'd been her biggest supporter even though she'd killed his child. She shuddered again.

"I didn't think I could do that, kill someone. Not even when he was there and Darcy was bleeding when my sister died. But when he tried to take you from me I couldn't see past him hurting you and me stopping him."

"I'm glad you did." He moved within inches of her without touching. "Alexis, I want you. Why don't we go back to the house and you let me show you just how much?"

Looking around the barn she realized that everything there could wait. And even if it didn't, she simply didn't care. Nodding to him, he picked her up and, before she knew it, he was taking them both to the shoreline where the waterfall was.

"You can't be serious. It's like fifty degrees out here."

He set her on her feet and pulled her into his arms. "I'll keep you warm. Plenty warm as soon as you're naked. Please take off your clothes and let me show you how warm I can really make you."

~~~

He didn't think she would. She looked ready to bolt back to either the house or the barn. Either way, he was going to chase her and take her. But when she stopped and started unbuttoning her shirt it was all he could do not to howl at the moon.

"Slower," he told her when she started pulling at the buttons quicker. "Take your time and let me savor the bare skin you expose for me."

"What about you? You going to be naked too or is it just going to be me?" She moved the buttons through the holes with ease now and her lower voice was doing all sort of things to his blood flow, especially heating it.

"You get naked and I'll show you how to strip for your mate. Would you like to know what I plan to do to you?" She closed her eyes and nodded. "I'm going to eat your pussy until you give me as much of your cum as I want. And I'm very hungry for you, so that could be quite a few times. Then I'm going to slowly enter you, filling you with my cock until I'm buried to the hilt. Would you like that?"

Her shirt fell from her fingers and onto the ground. The tiny bra she had on did nothing to hide her erect nipples and full breasts. His mouth watered at the thought of taking them into his mouth and suckling hard.

"Yes," she hissed as she moved her hands to the front of her bra. The clasp was undone in seconds and she teased him by leaving it there. When her hands slid down her belly to the top of her pants he knew she was trying to kill him.

The snap sounded in the deep forest, the zipper let go easily, slowly until he could see her panties along her abdomen. The lace hid from him his target. Dropping to his knees in front of her, he didn't touch her but watched.

"Take them off, Alexis. Take them off before I rip them from you and take you now." He licked his lips when she laughed softly. He looked up at her when her hands disappeared from her jeans.

"My breasts ache for you." She slid her hands under the lacey bra and cupped the bounty there. "My nipples are hard and long. I love it when you suck them. I could almost come when you do that."

"Alexis," he growled, and when he reached for her she stepped back. His wolf snarled for him to take, but he, the human male, loved her way of teasing him.

"Don't. You said you'd let me strip for you. I don't want to disappoint you by you going too fast. Watch me, Gordon. I want to make you want me."

He wasn't sure he could want her any more. But he put his hands on his thighs and hoped that he didn't hurt himself when he gripped himself too tightly. He leaned back on his heels and let her have her way...for now.

She leaned her head back as she enjoyed herself. Gordon was sure he'd never seen anything more erotic or beautiful as his mate standing there half-naked in the deep woods. As she slipped the bra down her arms and off his breath caught. Christ, she was going to kill him.

Full breasts and erect nipples bounced when she let them go and moved back to her pants. Her fingers danced along the top and then inside of the heavy fabric until she shimmied them down over her hips. He wasn't sure which he enjoyed more, her breasts jumping when she moved or the skin she was baring to him. When she struggled to get them off her legs he leaned in and she rested her hand on his shoulder and pulled them off her legs.

"Christ, you're beautiful. And mine." This time, when her hands went for her panties, he stayed her with a word.

"No. I want to taste you like this. I want to lick you slowly."

She nodded and watched through hooded eyes as he moved toward her on his knees. Touching her knees, he pulled them apart and steadied her. When she was inches from him Gordon leaned in and sniffed at her. Heaven, she smelled of heaven and sex.

"I'm not going to last. I thought that if I left my pants on I'd be able to pleasure you before I took what I wanted from you. But all I can think of is fucking you. Hard, fast, and claiming you." Her moan had him looking up from his vantage point of her soaking pussy. "Do you want me to take you, Alexis?"

When she stepped back he growled, but as soon as she turned and dropped to her knees in front of him, Gordon yanked at his jeans and tore the zipper and snap out. Her giggle had him smile.

"You won't think it is so funny to tease a wolf when you can't walk for a few hours." She leaned over onto her hands and presented him with her ass. "Alexis, I'm so sorry."

His cock leapt when he grabbed her hips. The heavy cream at the tip of his cock was nothing to the juices streaming down her thighs despite the lace. Tearing away the thong, the only thing keeping him from his goal, he fisted his cock and slammed into her.

Her climax screamed from her. When she begged him for more he leaned over her and took her hard. Stroke for stroke she met him; each thrust forward was met with a push back from her. When she tightened around his cock again, her walls milking him hard, he felt his own climax pulling from deep within him.

"Come in me, Gordon. Please, fill me with your seed and give me your child." Gordon knew she was in heat, he'd known for days it was close. "Please," she begged again before she threw back her head and howled out her release.

His wolf grabbed him and he felt the small shift hurtle through him. Canines dropped and he knew she was going to hurt, but he couldn't stop it any more than he could stop breathing. Nuzzling her shoulder, he licked the area between her neck and shoulder and bit her. Deep and hard, he sank his teeth as his climax hit him. As he held her still, claiming and marking her as his, he knew that they had created a child, their child, there in the dark woods.

# CHAPTER 21

Phil knew as soon as he was shown into the house that something had changed. It took him a few minutes to figure out what it was. There was laughter. Not just from one or two, but the whole house seemed to be in on a great joke. When he entered the kitchen, a place he knew that they spent most of their time, he stood watching them for a minute.

Sis was sitting on Gordon's lap. She looked so comfortable there he wondered if she was beginning to trust him more. She had a slice of apple in her hand and Phil watched as Gordon sliced another off the large, red apple in his own hand. Smiling, she took the offered piece as she popped the last one in her mouth.

Tim was sitting next to them. He was grinning, a big grin that showed that in the past week he'd managed to lose one of his front teeth. He too was enjoying an apple, only his was already on his plate sliced up. He leaned to his brother Jake and whispered in his ear. The other child laughed and stole a slice off his brother's plate.

Jake didn't say much when Phil had first come around. He seemed a great kid, but he knew from CJ that he possessed a very high IQ and had been tested recently. The results weren't back yet, but Phil was willing to bet that the kid was nearing genius status. Phil had found the kid reading encyclopedias on more than one occasion. He couldn't wait to tell Gordon he'd told him so.

Darcy was staring at him when he looked at her. Her smile was soft and reached her eyes. She'd changed the most. Everything about her showed her good health and well being. Phil had heard from Connor, Gordon's twin, that she'd talked more about the night her mother was killed. She had opened up to him, he said, because he'd let her see that a wolf could shift and not hurt. Phil thought she was a little in love with the wolf and hoped that Connor took a care where she was concerned.

"You should come in and join us." Phil looked over at Alexis when she spoke. "We have plenty of fruit to go around and there is homemade ice cream for later if you'd like to stay."

"I picked the berries all by myself," Tim chimed in. "Well, Jake and Darcy helped a little, but I did the...what did you call it, Gordon?"

"Toting. You did the toting. A real man totes his bounty home while the others gather. It's a good wolf who can provide for his family." Phil laughed when Alexis hit him. "Okay, it's a good wolf who can let his mate provide for him."

"Have a seat, Phil. I'll get you a plate so you can have something too." Alexis started to stand when Gordon beat her to it. The look between them made him look deeper into the woman and he was surprised by what he found.

"Congratulations are in order, I guess." Alexis flushed and Gordon puffed out his chest. "Would you like to know what it is?"

He could tell almost from conception what the sex of a baby would be. It was another of those odd quirks he got being a half-breed. He grinned at the two of them when she shook her head no and Gordon yes. Phil decided to hold off until they got more into their lives.

"Uncle Phil, did you know that Aunt Alexis and Gordon are gonna adapted us? We're not gonna be wolves, but we are going to be...." Sis looked confused for a second then brightened before she continued. "We're going to be a force to reckon with."

"I'm sure you already are, pumpkin," he told her. "And I believe you mean 'adopt' not 'adapted.'" She nodded and continued eating.

Gordon came back with a glass and a jug of tea. He set the empty plate in front of him before going back to his seat and picking up Sis. Looking around the table Phil thought of the things he had to tell them and the things that he needed answers for. First, though, he filled his plate with leftovers.

"You might as well spill it. Some of us have work to do." He looked up at Gordon as the kids left the room. "They have to clean their rooms and you look ready to bust. Say it."

"Okay. First and foremost, where is Holly? I need her. If she wants to bail on me, then I want to know. My family wants me to come back to Europe with them to live. I can't...I don't want to make Holly do this if she doesn't want to."

He held his breath while Alexis and Gordon looked at each other for several seconds. He could have looked into her mind, but decided not to. He wasn't sure what he'd find and was surer he didn't want to know.

"She's in New York. I don't know where other than the fancy hotel I told you about. Last time we heard from her she was buying something for a company. What, I don't know, but that's where she was as of last week." Gordon looked at Alexis again before continuing. "You need to claim her whether she wants it or not. She's your mate and that alone can do strange and sometimes terrible things to you if you don't claim each other."

"She doesn't sound like she's going to be easy, Phil," Alexis said with a huge grin. "I've never met her, but I'm pretty sure she comes by her last name naturally. I would say the 'take and conquer' approach is the best way for her."

"You don't care that she'll be pissed?" Phil was surprised by their shaking heads. "And if I tell her it was your idea, are you going to have to go into witness protection until she calms down?"

Gordon stood up and started gathering plates. "Not if you do it right, we won't."

# ABOUT THE AUTHOR

Kathi Barton, author of the bestselling series Force of Nature, lives in Nashport, Ohio with her husband Paul. In addition to writing full time Kathi likes to spend time with her eight grandkids, three children and three children-in-laws. She writes to relax and have fun.

Her muse, a cross between Jimmy Stewart and Hugh Jackman brings them to life for her readers in a way that has them coming back time and again for more. Her favorite genre is paranormal romance with a great deal of spice. You can visit Kathi on line and drop her an email if you'd like. She loves hearing from her fans. aaronskiss@gmail.com.

Follow Kathi on her blog:
http://kathisbartonauthor.blogspot.com/

www.ingramcontent.com/pod-product-compliance
Lightning Source LLC
Chambersburg PA
CBHW020607180626

46810CB00007B/2687